FIT
TO KILL

by Hans C. Owen

WILDSIDE PRESS

www.wildsidepress.com

This edition has been condensed slightly from the original, which was published under the title "Ways of Death."

THE PUBLIC WANTS TO KNOW

When the murder of Judge Somers and the mystery surrounding it was solved, the public was not given all the facts in the case. It was thought best at the time, in the interests of those most affected, to withhold many details which concerned only the private lives of innocent persons. This praiseworthy effort on the part of the authorities was, we now know, a mistake. The newspapers, particularly those that catered to the large mass of readers in the metropolitan areas, continued to hint at hidden evidence, police brutality and outright bribery. Covert allusions were made that only the wealth and position of those connected with the case, made it possible to conceal the truth.

The recent publication of an article in a popular magazine, which went so far as to intimate that a miscarriage of justice had been permitted, and that a searching investigation should be instituted, has prompted me to write the complete narrative of the amazing incidents which took place last spring and why murder, stark and retributive, swept through our peaceful community. The letters following herewith, will show the authority given me to publish the truth to the world.

FROM THE WIDOW:

```
"Dear Mr. Owen:
    Please do not hesitate to tell the
    complete story. Nothing that any one
    can do or say will soil my memories of
    my husband. His character and record
    not only in his public life, but in the
    unfortunate circumstances which led to
    his death, will always remain a living
    refutation to the slanders that may be
    cast up against him.
    As to my children and myself, we do not
    fear the publicity which may result
    from this intrusion into our privacy.
                    Cordially Yours
                    Marion Somers."
```

RADIO-GRAM FROM DEAN MATHER IN HONDURAS:

```
IF DEEMED BEST AND FAMILY WILLING, DO NOT
    CONSIDER ME.                    MATHER.
```

FROM EX-CHIEF LAWRENCE DONOVAN, SLIGO, IRELAND:

Dear sir:
 I have read the article referred to. I
was always opposed to secrecy. My
administration was on the level and the
publication of your story will prove
it. Why was it not done before?
                    Yours Truly
                        Lawrence Donovan.

FROM CHIEF OF POLICE SALVATORE CUSANI:

My Dear Mr. Owen:
 As far as I am concerned it makes little
difference whether or not you publish
the whole story. Leave me out of it as
much as you can. But don't spare us if
you think it necessary; we can take it.
What I can't see is why you want to
spill a lot of private history just to
satisfy a flock of old hens and morbid
sensation mongers.
                        Yours
                          S. Cusani.

FROM PERCIVAL TROUT:

Dear Owen:
 Open the closet and drag out the
cadaver. Let the Danse Macabre begin. I
think that you are worse than the public
which you excoriate in your hypocritical
letter to me. You know that nothing will
stop you from writing the story if you
can find a publisher, so what's the use
of asking my permission? Write the damn
stuff and get it off your chest.
                    Most amiably Yours
                          P. T.

I accept the mandate. These demands have made refusal impossible. The searching light of Truth points the way. *"LUX ET VERITAS."*

Young Bob Somers of the Junior class was a part of the University's traditions. His family for six generations had trod its ivy-covered halls. From the time when old Captain Eleazer Somers of Louisburg fame had laid the foundations of the family fortune, to the present, some grandparent, uncle or cousin was identified with it.

Judge Albert Somers, Bob's father, was one of the most distinguished of the alumni. He was a man of considerable wealth who had taken his profession seriously. From a young criminal lawyer, he had advanced to become an exceedingly capable district attorney of New York County and had succeeded to the bench after a brilliant career. He was fearless, honest, beyond taint of political intrigue and super-conscientious in anything pertaining to his work. He expected these same high standards and meticulous adherence to them in his associates. He was a member of the board of university trustees and a liberal dónor to the alumni fund. His crowning achievement was his recent gift of $200,000 for an archeological expedition to Honduras which was to be headed by his former classmate, the famous explorer and Quiche student William Mather, at present one of the deans of the university.

Back in the late nineties, Bert Somers and Bill Mather were inseparable. They had met at an exclusive preparatory school in New England and had gone down to the University together where they were room-mates for four years. They were both prominent in extra-curricular activities. Somers, the more aggressive, was the leader always, but Mather with his thoughtful and kindly consideration of others, was very popular. They were elected to the best clubs, played on the same athletic teams and, in the summer, spent their vacations together. When Somers married, a few years after graduation, Mather was his best man.

Mather remained at college doing post-graduate work and eventually became a member of the faculty. He remained a bachelor, devoting a great part of his time to Mayan research and exploration. It was to see him and go over the last details of the expedition that Judge Somers had come up from New York that day.

Bob met him at the railway station and they went to a hotel for lunch.

They had lighted cigarettes and were sipping their coffee.

"Your mother and sister send their love to you, Bob."

"Thanks, Dad. It's nice to see you again. Are you going to stay over this evening?"

"I had planned to take in Tap Day after my talk with Dean Mather," said the Judge.

"Why don't you use my room?" asked Bob. "It looks over the campus, just by the old elm. It's on the second floor. Dr. Mather's office is directly below it. Regular grandstand seat to see the failure and humiliation of your son and heir."

"Not nervous, are you, Bob?"

"Well, not exactly. You see I am a little worried on account of you. I know how badly you'd feel if 'H and C' didn't tap me. I don't see why they should anyway. I never was a star like you were during your time and I haven't set my heart on it like others have. Of course I'd be tickled pink if the miracle happened, but don't be disappointed if it does not."

"I won't," said the big, handsome Judge. "Don't worry; you'll come through all right. I think that we should be getting along. I have to go over the whole expedition with Mather and it will take all afternoon before we get through."

And thus the stage was set for an almost unbelievable drama.

At 5:55 P.M. young Bob Somers was standing with his fellow juniors waiting under the old elm.

Judge Somers was climbing the stairs from Mather's office to Bob's room directly above.

Mather was leaving by the door leading to his office and started to walk across the campus to his living quarters which were in the building about two hundred yards directly opposite on the west side of the quadrangle.

John Redfield, of the campus police, was guarding the east portal and chatting with patrolman Finn of the city police.

Chief Donovan was in his office a half mile away talking to detective-sergeant Salvatore Cusani and his assistant, Joe Blatchly.

Jim Romano, the dope pedler, was hiding behind the door of the entry to Dean Mather's office at the foot of the stairs.

President Davenport was in his office near the north portal checking over the honor list for the approaching commencement exercises and in the Chapel, the burly Professor Percival Trout was improvising on the pipe organ.

Thus were the pieces placed on the board when the long gray fingers of Death reached over and seized a pawn. The grim game commenced and moved on apace.

CHAPTER 1

T HE ENTIRE junior class, about seven hundred and fifty young men from many walks of life, was gathered around the old elm. The rest of the student body was standing beyond the roped off enclosure which held the juniors. It was a beautiful late afternoon in May. The well-kept campus lawn was fresh and green. The fine Gothic buildings on all four sides lent a sense of dignity and decorum to the scene. The ancient traditions of centuries past were reflected from their ivy-covered walls. The old university, which had sent many famous men into the world was about to enact one of its time-honored under-graduate customs.

Tap Day came annually on the last Thursday in May. This was the one hundred and third anniversary. The juniors, as was the custom, had gathered near the northeast corner of the oldest quadrangle. The portals leading into the campus through the buildings, were guarded by the campus police, an un-uniformed body of men whose duty it was to act as guides for visitors and aid the college officials in maintaining order when necessary. Today they were augmented by a squad of city patrolmen. No one was to be permitted into the quadrangle except faculty members, students and their invited guests. These guests occupied points of vantage at windows of the dormitory rooms which gave out on the scene. There was considerable speculation bandied about as to which of the juniors would be chosen by the five senior societies. The choice would fall on only ten percent of the class. Seventy-five men would feel the accolade. Many stories were dug up about former Tap Days. There was the old one, often denied but always revived, about a colorless and seedy junior who had been tapped by mistake by Hammer and Coffin; but as that junior after graduation became a great international figure, perhaps it was not a mistake after all.

Several of the under-classmen made slates of those they favored. This man would surely be tapped by H and C; that one by Knife and Fist; that one by Mask. On every list appeared the name of Bob Somers, class president and editor of the "Lit." He would be either the first or last for H and C, the oldest and most exclusive of the societies. The traditional usage gave the greatest honor to him who was tapped last, the next honor was to be the first chosen.

Bob watched the dean approach. The tall, lean, bronzed explorer flashed him a confident smile as he passed on his way across the campus. He looked up to the window of his room and saw his father taking his place there and waving him an assuring gesture. He

7

glanced about at his companions, slightly nervous.

The minute hand on the tower clock slowly approached the hour as Bob looked up again at the open window. His father was there smiling kindly and re-assuringly at him. The other windows of the buildings were filled with spectators; mothers, sisters and sweethearts in gay spring costumes. It was an inspiring scene and Bob felt a lump in his throat as a hush came over the assembly broken by the brazen clang of the great clock as it began to strike.

Every eye turned to the north-west portal. Then, while the reverberations of the last stroke were still heard, a man appeared walking rapidly. He was dressed in black and wore a black derby hat. He walked straight ahead toward the segregated juniors, brusquely brushing aside any one that stood in his way. It was Connors, the crew captain, out to make the first choice for H and C. He dove into the mass of juniors, pushing this way and that, searching for his man. He found him, stepped behind him and slapped him hard on the back.

"Go to your room," he shouted.

"First for Coffin!"

"Who was it?"

"Fletcher, I think; yes, there they go."

Fletcher hurried toward his dormitory followed by Connors. A cheer went up. It was a popular choice. Fletcher was the captain of next season's foot-ball team and well-liked. In the meantime other delegates had appeared on the scene from several entrances and more neophytes hurried away mostly with expressions of, "Great work," "Swell," and other congratulatory remarks shouted after them.

The tapping continued. Bob looked up at the window, but his father was not there. He thought that he saw him dimly at the back of the room. More than half of the choices had been made. His chances were getting slimmer. The man next to him, Barton of the polo team, was slapped and squeezed Bob's arm happily before he left. Bob glanced at the clock. It was 6:17. He looked up at his window again. His father was there and raised his hand to him in salute, smiling confidently. Bob gazed around; the seniors, still milling about, seeking the few chosen ones that remained. Of those some were disguising their chagrin with difficulty, others smiled bravely. Bob looked up again. It was 6:20. His father had left the window.

"He is disappointed and has given it up," thought Bob.

There was a commotion near him and as he dropped his eyes, he looked squarely into those of Tom Gregory, senior, captain of last year's championship football team, the biggest man in the university. Gregory stepped quickly in back of him and Bob felt a mighty whack between his shoulders while his ears rang to the stentorian command, "Go to your room."

Last man for H and C! Everybody cheered, for it was the most popular choice of the day. Confused and gloriously happy, Bob and Gregory fought their way through the struggling mass of their fellow students.

"Great work, H and C," "Good boy, Bob," "Swell," were some of the remarks shouted at them.

Many of his disappointed class-mates grabbed him and patted him on the back. It took several minutes before he could disentangle himself and break free. He hastened toward the door of his section, overtaking and passing Dean Mather who was returning to his office.

The dean smiled at him and whispered "Congratulations, Somers."

Bob, with Gregory close behind him, entered the section and hastily mounted the stairs. Just as Bob was about to enter the open door of his room, Gregory saw him stop and stiffen. Bob turned around with a look of horror and bewilderment on his boyish face. Gregory peered over Bob's shoulder and saw, sprawling on the floor, the inert body of Judge Albert Somers, a pool of blood forming under him.

CHAPTER 2

"HOLD ON," shouted Gregory throwing aside all tap-day dignity, "Brace up, Somers, I'm going to get the Dean." He called down the stairs, "Oh, Dr. Mather, will you please come up?"

The Dean had just entered through the outer section door and replied at once, "Certainly, Gregory, what is it?" and started leisurely up the stairs.

"Please hurry, sir, something dreadful has happened."

Mather took the last six steps in two and stood between the white faced boys gazing into the room.

"Good God!" he gasped, when he recognized the body of his friend.

He had seen death in many forms and knew that there was no hope here. He entered the room silently and knelt beside the body, placing his hand under the coat and feeling for the pulse merely as a matter of form. The flesh was still warm.

He rose, stepping back to avoid the soggy, blood soaked rug, and tripped over a black derby hat. He stooped, picked it up and dropped it casually on the near-by table. Turning to Bob, he said, "I am sorry, Somers, your father is dead. I think, Mr. Gregory, that you should take Bob over to your room. We will have to call the police at once."

"No, Dr. Mather, I am all right, thanks," said Bob. "I'll stay here with him."

"Stout fellow," said the Dean. "I will get some one right away. Stay where you are and do not touch anything." He looked at his watch. It was exactly half past six. He went down to his office and telephoned the city police-headquarters, reporting the case directly to Chief Donovan. He then telephoned to President Davenport and stepped out of the building and called to John Redfield, of the campus police, who was on guard at the east portal, and stationed him at the foot of the stairs with strict orders to allow no unauthorized person either in or out of the section.

He then ran quickly up the stairs and joined Bob and Gregory who were standing where he had left them on the upper landing.

When Redfield answered Dean Mather's call, he left patrolman Finn of the city police at the portal. Finn therefore, appeared greatly astonished when two squad cars came screaming up the street and with screeching brakes drew up in front of him. They spewed out the Chief, detective-sergeant Cusani, detective Blatchly, headquarters photographer, fingerprint expert, ballistic specialist and two uniformed policemen.

"Okay, Finn," said Donovan. "Where's the body?"

"What body, Chief?"

"The dead one, you fool."

"There ain't no dead body here, Chief."

"No? Why Professor Mather just called up and told us that Judge Somers of New York had been murdered, poor fellow, and you standing there and don't know anything about it. What in—"

"Just a minute, Chief. Johnny Redfield the campus guard, went in a few minutes ago. He said that Mather called him."

"Where did he go?"

Finn directed him to the section entrance and the Chief hastened toward it.

"Come on, Cusani, let's go."

"I'll join you in a minute," said Cusani. "I want to talk to Finn."

"Sally" Cusani was a smart, clever officer. He had enough imagination blended with native shrewdness and common sense to outguess and out-smart most of the criminals with whom he came in contact. He had had a great deal of experience in the Army Intelligence over seas after the armistice. He had recently made more than a local name for himself in the capture of a much-wanted gang of truck thieves. He turned to Finn.

Finn was a florid, blue eyed Celt. An old-timer who had never been promoted to any higher rating than patrolman, the old-fashioned cop who was content to remain in a rut, doing no more than his routine duties and careful not to exceed them lest he might get himself into deep waters. He was ready for his pension and had a good, if colorless, record.

"How long have you been here?" Cusani asked.

"I came on at three and I been here ever since."

"Notice any one go in or out?"

"Sure, all them students and some of their skirts."

"Anybody else?"

"Not until that Eyetalian came out."

"What Italian?"

"Well, just after Johnny Redfield left to go to that Mather guy, this here wop with a cut under his eye, comes running out here."

"Did you stop him? Who was he? Did you ever see him before?" asked Cusani tensely.

"I seen him before, sure. He's a stemmer. I don't know his name; a nifty dresser. He had on light brown pants and a coat like Dutch mustard, like them Willies at the collitch. You know."

"Yeah, I know. Was he wearing a hat?"

"He had one of them Al Smiths on."

"A brown one?"

"No, a black one."

"And he had a cut under his eye? Where did you ever see him before?"

"Around town, on the stem. I think the Chief had him up once. He was peddling numbers or something, but it didn't stick."

"And you didn't stop him?"

"No sergeant, I didn't."

"Okay. Wait here and keep your eyes peeled. Stop any one you don't know."

Dr. Mansfield, the medical examiner, drew his car up to the curb and accosted Cusani.

"Hello Sally. Is this the place?"

"Yes Doc, come on in. I'm just going up."

They entered the campus and turned to the right. When they had reached the section entry, Cusani waved the doctor up the stairs while he remained and confronted Redfield.

"What do you know about this?" he asked.

Redfield, a big blonde ruddy giant, recoiled slightly at Cusani's brusque inquiry, but braced himself with an effort as he replied, "I don't know anything. I don't even know who's killed. Dean Mather told me to keep unauthorized people out and your chief Donovan, asked me where the body was. Then, when I saw the medical examiner, I figured that some one was killed. That's all I know, sergeant."

Cusani looked at him coldly. "And you don't know who it was?"

"Why no. How was I to know?"

"Where were you when it happened?"

"Down at the portal."

"How do you know it happened when you were down there?"

"Because—Well I was down there all the afternoon." He stammered.

"You were down at the portal all afternoon? You are sure of that?"

"Why yes, sergeant—Sure I was there from noon until Dean Mather called me about half past six."

"Okay, stay here until I get you relieved. I want to see you later, so stick around."

The upper floor was crowded, but Donovan had allowed only the medical examiner, Blatchly, and the fingerprint man into the room with him. The others were standing, herded on the landing.

Dr. Mansfield was kneeling by the body, Joe Blatchly was prying about the room, the fingerprint man was spraying the furniture and Donovan was leaning against the table watching them. He was making sympathetic noises and murmuring, "The poor fellow. Ah, the poor fellow."

When he saw Cusani, he said: "Perhaps you'd better get these people in some other place Sally, and question them."

"You may use my office," volunteered the Dean. "It is the room immediately below this one."

"All right folks; will you two young fellows go with the Dean to his office? Officer Raff, there's a campus cop named Redfield at the foot of the stairs. Have him go with them and you stay down there at the door. I'll be down in a little while."

The Dean, Bob and Gregory trooped down with one of the uniformed police. Cusani entered the room as Dr. Mansfield was rising from his examination of the body.

Donovan looked at the doctor interrogatively. "Well?"

"He was shot all right, apparently from in front. The bullet passed through his heart and tore a hole in his back large enough to stick your fist in. He died probably at once and he was probably alive an hour ago. It's seven fifteen now so there you are. I don't think there's anything more to tell. If the coroner wants an autopsy, I'll do it, but I don't think that it will be necessary. I will report to him and let you have a copy of my report. That's all. If you need me you know where you can find me. They'll want the body at the morgue. Here's an order for its removal. I will examine it again to-night and try to figure out the angle the bullet took. It looks now as if it went through him almost horizontally."

When Dr. Mansfield had gone, Cusani asked Donovan, "Found anything?"

Chief Donovan shook his head mournfully. "No, Sally, not a thing, not a thing. No gun, no nothing. There's a hat on the table with a hole shot through it. He must have held it in front of him, the poor fellow."

"No, Chief, that doesn't follow. You don't know how many shots were fired. It may have been shot off his head at the first shot. Any prints, Elmer?"

"Sure, Sergeant, plenty. A few of the corpse's, a lot of the young fellow's and a couple of strange ones on that table. The Dean and the boy gave me theirs, on cards, out on the landing, and I took the ones off of the stiff before the Doc came in."

"You'll want some pictures taken, Sally," said Donovan. "Come in here, Melvin and take what the sergeant wants. I'm going back to headquarters. I'll leave everything in your hands, Sally. I don't have to tell you that this is the most important case we have ever been up against. I won't interfere with you. You can go right ahead; you won't need me. I'll send the morgue hearse for the remains. The poor fellow, äh the poor fellow." With a dolorous sigh the chief lumbered out.

Cusani glanced over at Blatchly. "Find the bullet yet?"

"No, but I know where it is. It's in the back of that chair."

He indicated an over-stuffed chair against the wall. A hole showed plainly in the leather-back. Probing about in the tear, he pulled out a bullet which had passed almost through the great thickness of leather and stuffing. He handed it to Cusani who after a brief examination passed it on to the ballistics man, saying "Now if we only had a .38 gun to match it, everything would be tied up nicely. Find any trace of another bullet, Joe?"

"No, and I don't think there's is another one, Sally."

"There should be. How else can you account for the one that went through the hat? . . . Well, perhaps he did hold it in front of him as the chief says, but . . . Okay. Let's get through with it. Go through his pockets, Joe."

Blatchly searched the dead man's clothes and soon a little pile of articles began to grow on the table. Two clean handkerchiefs, a platinum cigar case, a pigskin wallet, gold watch and chain, gold fountain pen and pencil. In the trouser pockets, a bunch of keys, two one dollar bills and some small change.

With Cusani's help, he turned the body over.

"Look at that!" he shouted as he pointed excitedly.

Protruding from the left hip pocket was the grip end of a heavy revolver.

"Keep your hands off it," cautioned the sergeant. "Here, Elmer, you take it and examine it for prints; when you're through, give it to Fred to match with the bullet. It's a .38, isn't it, Fred?"

"Yeah, Sergeant and one shot fired."

"Okay, boys take it along and make it snappy. I want a report as soon as you can give it to me." He turned to Blatchly "Let's go through the wallet."

The wallet was practically empty. A pilot and driver's license was all they found. They were made out in Somers' name.

Cusani stood silently pondering for several minutes. He picked up the hat from the table and examined it carefully. There was a large ragged hole on each side of it. The inside was unlined save for the label of a local furnisher and the initials, "J.R." in gilt letters pasted in.

"J.R." mused the sergeant. "That might be John Redfield. How did his hat get up here?" He turned to Blatchly "I guess that will be about all up here for now. I'm going to talk to those fellows down stairs and get the whole story. Maloney, you stay with the body and when the morgue people come for it, let them take it away. Wait here for me and don't let anyone else in. Don't touch anything."

CHAPTER 3

SERGEANT CUSANI and Detective Blatchly entered the Dean's office. Seated there, on one side of a table, were Dean Mather, Bob Somers and Gregory. In a corner of the room sat Redfield. At the other side of the table was an authorative looking middle aged man whom Cusani recognized as President Davenport of the University and beside him sat Percival Trout M.D., Ph.D., D.Sc., LL.D. Contab., D.C.L.Oxon., Officer of The Legion of Honor, Croix de Guerre with two Palms, D.S.O., Dean of the School of Psychology and probably the most distinguished person in the University. He was built on generous lines with immense shoulders, rather short neck and a huge round head, almost entirely bald. He wore a heavy blue-black moustache. His features were coarse and rough-hewn; his eyes, a light china blue. He looked more like a stereotype cartoon of a political ward boss than the famous scientist and world-renowned savant that he was.

Cusani, dapper and efficient, stood in the doorway scanning the assembly for a moment, after which he walked in briskly, followed by Blatchly. He nodded respectfully to President Davenport who rose and said: "Dr. Mather telephoned to me about this tragic affair and I came over as soon as I could find Dr. Trout. I thought it best to have him with us. This is Dr. Trout here, Sergeant, perhaps you have met him before."

"Yeah, I've known him since I was a kid. I was in the old third ward school when he went to high school. Everybody knows 'Butch' Trout. The local boy who made good. Besides that, he's our town war hero and—"

"Lay off, Sally. Can it," squeaked Trout in a startlingly piercing falsetto, a broad grin transfiguring his ugly face as he flashed his strong, white teeth. "Dr. Davenport is not interested in the least. He thought that with my experience in the Army Intelligence and the lucky breaks I've had since, in matters of this kind, I might be of help to you."

"I know that you can be of help to me and I can use help now. It won't be the first time that you've helped me out. There is something damn screwy about this case that I don't understand. I want to get all the facts and help I can. You can all help me. Perhaps you, Dean Mather, had better tell me what you know about this."

"Well," said the Dean slowly, "there's not very much to tell. I had left Judge Somers in this office while I went over to my living quarters across the campus. The time was a few minutes before six. I wanted to get some data for him about the Honduras expedition. It took me some time to find what I wanted—some recent meteorological charts. As it was, I didn't find them all and I recall now that I had sent them to the Hondurian legation in Washington for corrections. When I came back here, Mr. Gregory and young Mr. Somers overtook me a short distance from the outer section door. They entered the building first. As I was about to follow I heard them calling me from above. I entered, went up and found them on the landing looking into the room. When I saw the Judge lying there, I rushed in and felt his heart and pulse. He was quite dead. The body was still warm. It could not have happened more than a few minutes before we arrived. I left the boys on the landing and summoned help at once."

"Thanks, Dr. Mather. Is that all? You didn't search the room?"

"No, I didn't. I thought it best to get the authorities without delay."

"Thanks," said Cusani, "I wish everybody felt like that. Our jobs would be much easier." He turned to the two students and asked, "Which of you is Mr. Somers?"

"I am," said Bob, looking up miserably.

"Thanks, Mr. Somers. I am sorry about this thing and I won't keep you long. Please tell me all you know about it. Did you see your father to-day before he met the Dean?"

"Yes, I had luncheon with him at the hotel."

"Okay. Start from there and tell me everything you did and he did, until the time you found him upstairs. Take your time, Mr. Somers, remember I wouldn't trouble you if it wasn't necessary. I've got a job to do. Perhaps you can help me."

Bob, after a few moments' thought, told what had happened that afternoon. A very clear cut and concise narrative.

"Thanks," said Cusani, "your story will save me a lot of work. Mind answering a few questions?"

"Of course not," said Bob.

"Did you or your father pay for the luncheon at the hotel?"

"Why, father did."

"Thanks. Do you remember how much the bill came to?"

"Not exactly. We didn't eat much. I remember that dad received several dollars and some silver in change from a five dollar bill." He seemed a bit bewildered. The others looked at Cusani wondering what that had to do with the Judge's death.

Trout alone seemed to grasp that this questioning was of importance and watched the detective sharply.

"That's fine, Mr. Somers," said the sergeant. "Now, think carefully, when your father gave the waiter that five dollar bill, had he taken it from his pocket or from a pocket-book?"

"Why—I don't remember," answered Bob, looking at the tense eager face of the sergeant. "Let me think—it seems to me—why yes of course—He took it out of his wallet with a bunch of other bills, mostly tens and twenties. He always carried a few hundred dollars with him."

"Thanks," said Cusani with a grim smile. "Now when you were waiting out there on the campus, did you notice whether or not your father was wearing his hat up there at the window?"

"Yes, sir, I am sure he was because he waved it at me once."

"Are you absolutely sure of that, Mr. Somers? What kind of hat was it?"

"A black derby. Now, that you mentioned it, perhaps he did not have it on all the time. I seem to have an impression, rather vague, that I saw him without it also."

"Thanks. You don't know whether it was earlier or later that you saw him without the hat? It might be important."

Bob thought hard a moment before he answered "No. I can't say, Sergeant. Sorry."

"That's okay. Did your father carry a gun?"

"No—at least I don't think so—In fact I am sure that he did not."

"What makes you so sure?"

"Well, he had been getting threatening letters recently and some of his friends had suggested that he carry a revolver for protection. He made light of the threats and grew quite indignant about the revolver. He was always opposed to anything of that kind."

"You say that he had received some threatening letters recently? Do you know from whom and what they were about?" asked Cusani, making no effort to mask his eagerness.

"No I don't," said Bob. "He made light of them, saying that all men in positions similar to his were targets for that sort of thing. It didn't frighten him any."

"I think that's all, Mr. Somers. Thank you very much and unless Mr. Gregory can add anything to your statements, you can both go. Your father's body will be held until to-morrow."

"Can you tell me what happened, sergeant?" asked Bob.

"I don't know. He was shot. By whom and how I can't say. We have the gun and the bullet. I will keep in touch with you. Good night—Oh, by the way—did your father buy his hats here or in New York?"

"Father had his hats made by a private hatter in New York."

"Thanks," said Cusani. "Good night again." He stroked his chin thoughtfully, considering his next step. He glanced up quickly as Redfield came stumbling out of the corner. The big guard's face, usually ruddy, was ashen; his blue eyes stricken with fear.

"Well, I guess I'll be going too, sergeant," he mumbled.

"Why?"

"Why? Because—because I'm hungry." Redfield forced a sickly smile.

"Just a minute. Is there anything you can add to what you told me a little while ago?"

"Not a thing, Sarge. Not a thing," Redfield answered a little more confidently.

"Let's see that hat you are holding," snapped Cusani.

Redfield recoiled and quavered, "Hat? What hat?"

"The one you have in your hand. Hand it over."

Redfield tried to smile but made a miserable job of it as he stammered, "Well, Sergeant, you see it . . . it isn't mine . . . I . . . I . . . I just picked it up . . . here . . . in this room. I don't know whose it is . . . I don't know . . . I don't know where mine is . . . I . . . ."

"Give me that hat!" barked Cusani.

Redfield looked about wildly, like a trapped animal, but surrendered the hat to the sergeant.

Cusani examined it carefully and smiled grimly. He looked at the big guard triumphantly and said, "So you don't know whose hat it is, eh? Let me read what it says in the lining and you'll get an idea. 'Made for A. Somers Esq., by Rudolph Shuler New York City.' The Judge's hat! . . . What have you got to say for yourself now, Redfield?"

Redfield made no reply.

"Not talking eh?" sneered Cusani. "Well, we'll give you a chance to think it over. Take him to the station Joe and lock him up. I'll be over in a little while."

When Blatchly had departed with his dejected prisoner, President Davenport said gently, "But why all this excitement? What if it was Judge Somers' hat? He may have left it in this room when he went upstairs and Redfield picked it up where he had left it just now. Don't you think so, Dr. Trout?"

Cusani interrupted before Trout had a chance to reply.

"Yeah, he might have, but he didn't. You see that phony cop had that hat on when I sent him in here."

He paced up and down the room for a minute then turned abruptly.

"Well, I guess that's all for now, gents. May I use your phone, Dean?"

While Cusani was telephoning, President Davenport excused himself after talking to Trout and Mather. Cusani at the telephone watched him as he went out. He had a talk with Chief Donovan, left some instructions and received some reports. He rose and said, "I am going up stairs again. I haven't had a chance to look over the room carefully. Come up if you like, Major Trout. I'd like to get your slant on this thing."

Trout followed Cusani up the stairs. For a man of his size and weight he was exceedingly agile. They found Patrolman Maloney on guard who told them that no one except the men from the morgue had been there.

"Okay," said Cusani, "Give me the keys and you can go. Tell old Finn at the portal to wait a few minutes for me."

Maloney nodded and trudged off.

As he was unlocking the door Cusani looked at Trout and smiled uncomfortably but it was not until they were in the room with the door closed and locked that he said, "Look here, Major, I suppose that President Davenport dragged you into this to safeguard the university's reputation. Personally I have no objections, in fact I welcome your assistance. But I want to get some things off my chest first. Let's get this straight. No matter who it is that may be suspected, I am not going to do any covering up. No matter what lies behind this killing, I am going to drag it out." He paused, then continued as though choosing his words with care. "I appreciate your ability, Major. No one who has worked with you as I did in France after the armistice can deny your fine deductive powers and I hope that you will allow me to consult you whenever I need help."

"Of course, Sally," said Trout good-naturedly. "Call on me whenever you like. I see what you are driving at. Our stations are reversed. The situation is different. In France I was the one on whom the responsibility rested. Here it is on you. This is your case. You need not tell me anything more."

"That's okay then," said Cusani with a boyish grin. "After all this may be all clear sailing from now on. Redfield is on the spot."

Trout grunted and asked "Would it be too much to ask, Sergeant, just what you have on Redfield beside the fact that he was wearing Judge Somers' hat?"

"Don't be so damned formal, Butch. We're going to work this out together. You can see that Redfield must have been in this room sometime this afternoon or evening. His hat is there on the table and he had the Judge's hat on when he tried to get away. I want to find out why and how he killed the judge."

"If he did," interpolated Trout.

"Yeah, if he did," repeated Cusani. "Anyway he is our hottest suspect at present. Sit down on that window-seat over there, Percy. I am going over this room with a fine toothed comb."

He hesitated a moment, then continued, "I might as well put you wise to the lay-out. The body was lying right there. Feet to the window and head in the doorway which leads to the bedroom. Those things on the table are from his pockets. The bullet which I told you about came out of the back of that leather chair and that hat with the hole through it on the table is Redfield's."

Trout nodded. Cusani walked slowly around the room, looked out of the window, stirred up the ashes in the fireplace, stopped and picked up a small article on the rug, returned to the fireplace and examined it carefully and then went through the door into the bedroom and bathroom where he remained a short while.

While he was gone, Trout walked over to the entrance door and faced the room at several angles, repeating the same performance at the bedroom door. He picked up the damaged hat on the table examined it carefully and replaced it meticulously, shaking his head. He returned to the window-seat and scrutinized the hangings, sat down and glanced over at the table. Then taking a piece of paper from his pocket he made a rough sketch of the room and its contents. At that moment Cusani came in from the bedroom. The Sergeant seemed pleased with what he had discovered.

"Here," he said, "is a chip of brick. It came from the back of the fireplace. You can see the new red scar it left against the soot. Like a red carnation on an undertaker. It may have something to do with the case. And here is a gold ring I found on the rim of the wash-bowl in the bathroom. What do you make out of that?" As he spoke, he passed the ring over to Trout.

"It's the Judge's ring, Sally. His class ring, 1912. There's something on it that looks like blood. Better take it to the laboratory and have it checked. . . . In the bathroom? . . . And that nick in the back of the fireplace and that damn hat on the table. To use one of your very expressive colloquialisms, the whole thing looks cock-eyed to me, but then I don't know how much you know."

"Not too much. I may tell you later. I'm going over to the station and see what they have found out and talk to that Redfield guy."

Trout accompanied him to the portal where Patrolman Finn was waiting patiently.

"Thanks for waiting, Pat," said Cusani with his infectious smile which had made him so popular on the force. "I just wanted to check up on Redfield again. Was he wearing a hat?"

"Sure he was . . . A black dip . . . If that's all I'll be going. I'm late to me dinner." He stopped a moment aghast then shouted, "Holy Mother, it's Thursday night! Red Mike and Violets!" and dashed off at an amazing speed.

"What is Red Mike and Violets?" asked Trout.

"Corned beef and cabbage," explained Cusani.

Trout watched the departing officer with a smile and turned to Cusani, "Well, he evidently is fond of it. But he has reminded me that I too need some nourishment. How about joining me, Sally?"

"No, thanks, Major," Cusani said, then he added, "I would like to talk to you again tonight. Will it be okay if I drop in to see you later? That chip from the fireplace and the ring have given me a lot to think about. If the chip was made by a bullet, another shot must have been fired. If so, where is that bullet? If the Judge left the ring on the washbowl, he must have been interrupted by somebody while he was washing his hands. Why was he washing his hands at that time? Who interrupted him? Let's give that some thought and we will talk it over when I see you later. Okay?"

CHAPTER 4

WHEN SERGEANT CUSANI entered his office at headquarters he found that Chief Donovan had gone for the night. Blatchly was waiting for him, and greeted him impatiently.

"Say, Sergeant, that Redfield bird is a dummy. He don't know how to talk. The chief and I had him up ever since he got here. I wanted to take him down in the cellar, but you know the chief . . . too damn soft-hearted."

"Yeah and you know me, too, Joe. There'll be no rough stuff. What did Elmer and Fred find?"

"I don't know. They wouldn't tell me nothing. They're waiting to report to you. I'm only one of the help around here."

Cusani smiled. "Tell them to come in," he said.

The fingerprint expert and the ballistician had completed their examination. Several fingerprints besides those of Judge Somers had been found on the weapon, but there was no record of them in the local files.

"How about Redfield, Elmer?" asked Cusani.

"Nothing like his, Sergeant. No, they are strange ones. Very distinctive. I ain't never seen them before."

"Wire them to Washington. Hoover's boys may have seen them." He turned to the other expert who was waiting with a complacent smile. "How about the gun and the bullet? Did you find anything?"

"Plenty, Sergeant. The bullet was fired from that gun all right. There's no question about it. The gun is almost brand new, too, and here is a piece of luck for you . . . We've traced the gun already."

"Good boy, Fred. That's fast work. Whose is it?"

"Well I don't know who had it today, but you remember that break-in at the Bartlett Hardware Company last fall? Well I had a list of all the guns that were stolen then. There was six of them and this had the serial number of one of them."

Cusani dismissed him with a word of praise and turned to Blatchly.

"What do you think of that, Joe?" he asked.

"It's a cinch," said the stout detective. "Redfield, of course. A local gun, a local killing, a local man. You can't get around it."

"Do you think that he broke into the hardware store too?"

"He didn't have to, Sally. He could of bought it from the guy that did, couldn't he?"

"How about those fingerprints?"

"Fingerprints is a lot of hooey. I ain't never seen no one hanged on fingerprints yet."

"How do you account for the gun being in the Judge's pocket?"

"Redfield had to get rid of it, didn't he? Show me a better place to put it—"

"Thanks, Joe," interrupted Cusani. "That's very illuminating now. The way you figure it is that Redfield went up to that room, killed the Judge, took his money, then slipped the gun into the Judge's hip pocket and turned him on his back without leaving any prints on the gun. Is that it?"

"Yeah, something like that."

"Did you search Redfield?"

"Sure. He didn't have nothing incriminating on him."

"A pair of gloves maybe?"

"No, nothing like that. A pack of cigarettes and some papers and letters, a dollar bill and some change. That's all."

"Okay, Joe, bring him in. I'll talk to him."

Blatchly brought the prisoner into Cusani's office. The Sergeant greeted him pleasantly.

"Sit down, Redfield. Have a cigarette? I'm going to ask you to help me."

The big fellow looked around suspiciously and hesitated. Then, picking a cigarette from the proffered packet, sat down.

"You see," continued Cusani, "I've got a tough job ahead of me. Somebody murdered Judge Somers. My job is to find out who did it. If you did it, you might as well confess right now. It will be easier for you in the long run. If you want a lawyer to take care of your interests you have the privilege of getting one. I want to be fair with you. What do you say?"

"I don't want a lawyer, Cusani. I haven't done anything wrong ... You let me go ... I might be able to help you find the right man. I want to help."

"How did your hat get mixed up with Judge Somers'?"

"I don't know. Honestly ... I picked that hat up in Dean Mather's office where you saw me."

"Then what became of the hat you were wearing when you went into that office?"

"I don't know. If it isn't there now, some one else must have taken it out."

"Not so good, Redfield. You were not wearing your hat when you went into Dean Mather's office because your hat was lying on the table upstairs with a bullet hole in it. It was up there, Redfield, in the room where Judge Somers was killed," said Cusani quietly. "Perhaps you can explain that too?"

Redfield looked up with panicky fear in his blue eyes and started to speak, but stopped and sank back into his chair silently.

"Well, Redfield, what about it?" urged Cusani.

Redfield remained silent.

"What were you doing in that room?"

"I wasn't there," blurted Redfield.

"Your hat was up there."

Redfield looked worried and cast nervous glances at the two policemen.

"Come on Redfield, why did you kill him?"

"I didn't ... I didn't ... I don't know anything about it ... You leave me alone," he shouted hysterically. "Let me out of here ... You are trying to scare me ... Leave me alone ... I know all about you cops ... You're going to needle me ..."

"Shut up, you fool! No one is going to hurt you. I told you you could get a lawyer. Take it easy now and answer me if you want to. You said that you might be able to help me. Finn says that he saw some one running out of the campus. A wop, he said, that looked as if he had been in a fight. Did you see him too?"

"Yes. That was just before Dean Mather called me."

"Recognize him?"

"I've seen him about town. He's a tough guy and hangs about the college. I think he sells booze to the students."

"Do you know his name?"

"I don't know his whole name. They call him 'Jimmy the Wop'. "

"Okay Joe, take him back. No one is going to hurt you, Redfield," Cusani added as the big hulk looked fearfully at Blatchly.

When they had gone, Cusani called up the medical examiner with whom he held a long conversation. Then he made some notes and compared them with the data he had jotted down in Dean Mather's office. He could arrive at no conclusion. There were too many clues and most of them seemed to contradict each other. The bullet in the back of the chair had gone through a thick layer of felt and upholstery and was practically intact. Could that bullet have gone through a man's body and still have force enough to penetrate so deeply that thick, tough material? If that bullet had hit the back of the fireplace, could it have ricocheted and still retain its shape?

Could that bullet have gone through the hat that was lying on the table?

What was the revolver that fired that bullet doing in the Judge's hip pocket?

Who had taken the Judge's money?

What was the Judge's ring with blood on it doing in the back room?

Who was the man with the cut on his face?

Did Finn and Redfield actually see such a person?

Had he been cut by the Judge's ring?

If so, what was he doing in that room?

Redfield's hat? The Judge's hat?

Who did it?

Blatchly knocked at the door, "Say, Sergeant, do you know what time it is? I ain't had nothing to eat and it's after nine o'clock."

Cusani smiled. "Well, Joe, they say that an empty stomach induces clear thinking. Sit down and tell me what your reaction is to Redfield."

"Perhaps he didn't do it."

"How about the hat?"

"He might of told the truth. He didn't have the Judge's roll on him. The guy what croaked the Judge lifted the dough, didn't he?"

"Well, if Redfield didn't do it, who do you think did, Joe?"

"There's his son; then there is that high hat Mather guy and the other young fellow. They was the first there. We didn't search them. The son admitted that he knew his old man had the roll. Perhaps he and the other guy . . ."

"No, Joe, why should . . ."

"Churche the fam, Sally. Churche the fam." Blatchly waved his hand airily.

Cusani smiled. "You may be right at that, Joe. We may find a woman at the bottom of it."

"Well," said Blatchly, ponderously, "I have given you my ideas, now you tell who you think did it?" And he sat back in his chair in a judicial pose.

"I don't know, Joe. I agree with you on Redfield. I don't think he could have done it and disposed of the money in such a short time. In fact I doubt very much if he was anywhere near the scene when the killing took place. But, on the other hand, there is his hat to be explained . . . I would like to know more about the fellow with the cut on his face. He seems to fit in much better."

"Yeah, I think he's the one, Sergeant."

"I thought you said it was the son?"

"It might of been."

"How about Finn?"

"Sure, Sergeant," Blatchly laughed, "Old Pat did it."

Cusani smiled. "Well, I am considering him too. Let's see now. There's Finn . . . He was at the gate and on the campus during the whole show. So, maybe, was Redfield. Then there was young Somers and Gregory, they were in the room, or at least in the doorway on their own statements and they give each other an alibi. Then there is Dean Mather who was in the room. But he was there with the two young fellows . . . He might have done it before, so I am not dismissing him either. Now who else was there?"

"There's President Davenport and Doc Trout, Sergeant."

"Hell, yes. They were there and so were about five thousand others near there. This is not going to get us anywhere, Joe. What we've got to find is a motive."

"We've got that . . . The Judge's roll."

"Yes, that is missing, but not his expensive watch, nor his platinum cigar case nor his ring nor . . ."

"I've got it," interrupted Blatchly jubilantly.

"Well?"

"It's that guy with the cut face. You know, the wop that Finn and Redfield saw. He goes up and holds up the Judge and the Judge hands over the dough. Then he sees the Judge's watch and makes a grab for it. Then the Judge hits him and cuts his face with the ring. The guy pops him with the gat and when he sees that he has croaked him, he gets scared and beats it with the dough. That's what happened, Sally."

"Do you think so, Joe? And then the Judge puts the wallet back in his pocket, picks up the gun, puts that in his hip pocket, walks into the bathroom and leaves his ring there, goes back to the front room and makes a hole in a hat and lies down and dies. Is that what you mean, Joe?"

"No, Sergeant. But I still think the cut-faced guy did it. Perhaps I can't think so well on an empty stomach after all. Okay to get a bite now?"

"Yes, get your supper. I am going to the college again. If anything turns up, call me at Prof. Trout's office. Oh and by the way, Joe, when you get your supper eat plenty of fish. The trouble with you isn't an empty stomach. So long."

CHAPTER 5

TROUT GREETED Cusani cordially. Dean Mather was seated with him at the table in his office. Trout had provided a tray of sandwiches and some old Scot's whisky and soda.

"Come on, Sally! 'Fall to,' as the immortal Sammy said."

"Thanks and thanks again, Major," said the hungry Cusani. "That's exactly what I needed."

"Knowing you as I do and that 'uncompromising disposition' of yours I was sure you would turn up tired and hungry. When you have all you want, we will listen to what you have to tell us. I asked Mather to join us as he may be able to check up on some of our data seeing that he was one of the first on the job. Hope you don't mind."

"That's okay," mumbled Sally, his mouth full of sandwich. "I'm glad to get all the help I can."

Trout mixed some drinks and Mather lighted his pipe. Cusani glanced at the two deans. They made a strange contrast. Mather tall, lithe and blond; Trout heavy, broad and dark. But both gifted with extraordinary intelligence. He felt a little uneasy at first in Mather's presence. He knew something of the man's background. An aristocrat to his finger-tips, descended from a long line of cultured forefathers; a man of wealth and position . . . With Trout, of course, it was different. He himself had seen the Major rise from lowly surroundings and had had frequent contacts with him. In fact Cusani felt that he owned much to Percival Trout. What few cultural attainments he had acquired were due to Trout's influence. Cusani was ambitious and not only willing, but anxious, to advance himself. He saw what Trout had done and had for years, set the Major as an example to follow.

He brushed a few crumbs from his coat, lighted a cigarette and refilled his glass. He looked up and smiled.

"That was great. I feel like a new man, Percy, and now let's hear what you make of this murder."

"You want me to tell you?" asked Trout.

"Sure; you heard me examine the witnesses and saw me search the room. I am surprised that you haven't turned the guilty one over to me yet. What's the matter? Are you losing your cunning, Doctor? You know that you love a good audience. Why the reluctance now?"

"So that's it, is it? You eat my food and drink my whisky and now you want to pick my brain too. Really, Mather, I think it would serve this wise-cracking dago right if we left him in the lurch ... But, I feel that something must be done to clear up this case and I know that this poor nitwit can't get along without my help so without any assistance from him, here is the story. Check me up if you think I am wrong."

Trout took a long pull from his glass and set it down slowly and continued. "According to Mather and confirmed by young Somers, the Judge walked up the stairs to the room at five minutes before six. He appeared at the window a minute afterward. He was there at a minute before six; both of these times checked from Bob's statement. At six the first man to start the tapping entered the quadrangle. Between 6:07 and 6:13 the Judge had left the window. This is from Bob's statement. You will remember he kept looking at the clock."

"At 6:15 he was there again, but at 6:20 he was gone. At about 6:25 the body was found. At 6:27 Mather was in the room and at 6:30 he was telephoning to the police. Is that time schedule correct?"

"Perfect, Prof. Trout," said Cusani. "But how you—"

"Shut up. If you had my brains, even you might amount to something," squealed Trout. "Now then— From this it is evident that he was killed somewhere between 6:20 and 6:25, when the body was found. Right?"

"Marvelous, Dr. Priestdyke," interjected the Sergeant. "What a brain!".

" 'That is the worst of country service,' " quoted Trout. " 'The juniors is always so very savage.' Now if you will exercise your little 'gray cells,' if you have any, and grovel around for a few pearls instead of perpetrating the diosmosetic emanations of a bicronic cerebrum on your betters, I will proceed. I said that the murder was committed between 6:20 and 6:25. I think that we may cut the time shorter than that because Bob, Gregory and Mather were approaching the door of the section and did not see any one go out. There was no one in the rooms. Let's chop off two more minutes. He was killed between 6:20 and 6:23. Three minutes. That's agreed? Now then— He had two visitors while he was up there; maybe three but I am not sure of the third yet. One of them shot at him; the other walked out with his money and maybe something else. The one that shot at him missed him. I have a pretty good idea but no proof, as to who took the money. Who shot at him, I don't know yet until I hear what Sally has to say. But I can tell you this— He was killed after the two visitors left and they had nothing to do with the murder. How's the Vanity holding out, Sally?"

"I've got to hand it to you, Major," he said as he pushed the bottle along. "You're a wonder."

Mather stared at his fellow dean with admiration written on his lean bronzed face. "How did you get all that, Percy?" he asked.

"Elementary, my dear Watson," squeaked Trout delightedly. "You know my methods. Apply them. And now, insect," turning to Cusani, "loosen up. Tell me about the gun and the bullet."

"Okay, smart guy. Here's where you get a bump. The gun was in his hip pocket."

"In whose hip pocket?"

"In the Judge's, Philo Queen. Let's hear you deduce that one off."

"That clinches it then," shrilled Trout. "That makes it practically perfect. The gun in his hip pocket, eh? And only one cartridge discharged I'll wager. Did your ballistics man match the bullet and the gun? They fitted, didn't they? Eh? And the Judge never owned a gun. Did he? It was some one else's, wasn't it? Do you know whose it was? Were there fingerprints on it? The Judge's of course; any others? Eh? Come across, Sally."

"But look here, Trout," interjected the Dean. "You couldn't know it was not his gun. It could have been suicide."

"Really, Mather, you astound me. Suicide is impossible for at least three excellent reasons. First, if Sally thought it was, he would not be wasting my time. Second, the shot that killed him was not fired from that gun. Third, if he did commit suicide, where is the weapon that did it and where is the bullet? I am right, am I not, Sally, when I say that there were no powder marks or burns on his clothes? You see, if a man shoots himself through the heart, he can't hold the weapon far off. Try it and see. It's an awkward position. Moreover why should one committing suicide adopt a contortive attitude? He'd want it over and done with as soon as possible. He wasn't killed by that gun, because the bullet was found in a place which had no relation to the body. It went through thick leather and felt, a much greater distance than a revolver bullet could have traveled after going through a human body. Besides that, the Judge was a tall man and Mansfield says that the missile passed through him horizontally. In that case it could not have lodged in the back of that chair. Anyway if that gun had killed him, it would not be in his pocket. No! Suicide is out. Now, Sally, tell us all about the gun and the bullet."

"My hat is off to you, my dear Doctor," said Cusani smiling. "But I am afraid that you have jumped to conclusions a little too quickly this time."

"Of course, if you have been holding out on me—"

"No. I wanted to see how far you would go," said the detective.

"Now let's get down to something practical. I, too, think that the suicide theory can be washed out of the picture. Judge Somers was murdered all right and I expect to be able to tell you by whom before many hours. You see, we have already traced the gun. It's a local affair. It is one of those which were stolen from the Bartlett Hardware Company last fall. We had all the serial numbers and this was one of them. Now the Judge, as far as we know, had no contact with any local gangsters. There can be only one solution. He was killed for his money.

"No—wait a minute, gents. You want to know how the rod got into his pocket? True, that is hard to get around, but not impossible. I had a talk with Doc Mansfield on the phone and he admits that there might be a possibility."

"A possibility of what?" piped the exasperated Trout.

"Well, this is the way I think it happened," continued the unperturbed Sergeant. "There was a struggle for the gun and it was fired while the Judge was holding it and he slipped it into his pocket. It wouldn't take more than a second. A sort of a reflex action I think he called it. It is possible that he might have lived a second and done that. Anyway Doc said that it could have happened although it was very unlikely." He glanced challengingly at his two astonished listeners and continued. "In cases of this kind we must consider the unlikely as well as the apparent. You taught me that yourself, Major. We know that Judge Somers had a roll and we also know that that roll is now missing. We know that the weapon used was a stolen one. From that, it doesn't take much brains to deduce a criminal and a stick-up. Knowing what we do of the Judge's character, we can take it that he would be the last man to meekly surrender his money on demand. He made a fight for it. The gun was in his hand when it went off. That I can prove. He had powder marks on his cuff.

"Just a minute more and you can do your deducing. Yes, the gun fired the bullet that we found and that was the only bullet in the room. Yes, there were other finger-prints on the gun, the same as those on the table. We have wired them to Washington. We should get an answer before noon tomorrow. Those boys are good and fast. I have got the description of a possibility that may fill the bill. He was seen to leave the campus in a hurry at about the time the killing was done. He had the marks on him of having been in a fight. One of our harness bulls saw him. We have some lines out on him now. After all, it's just a common thug-killing and nothing mysterious about it."

Cusani leaned back in his chair and tossed off his glass of whisky, eyeing Trout over it. He then turned to Mather and said, "Poor old Major, he can't take it."

Trout snorted contemptuously. "So that is your idea of something practical. If I hadn't known you for many years, Sally, me lad, I might fall for your story and believe that you also believe that tripe. But I don't believe it and neither do you."

"But I do, seriously. What's the matter with it? Not enough mystery to suit you?"

"What's wrong with it, Trout?" asked Mather.

"What's wrong with it?" squealed Trout. "Why the damn fool should have his head examined. 'Not enough mystery' indeed! He has injected more mystery in this asinine hypothesis than Mazuriak did in his theory of the bionomic propagation of opsonic cploriasms."

"Yeah, that's right," laughed Cusani, "go on call me names. Come on now, tell us where I am wrong."

"I have no more time to waste on you. It is almost mid-night and I have two lectures to give in the morning. More pearl casting. I am going to take a walk around the quadrangle and turn in."

He rose heavily, took up his hat and walked out followed by the others.

During the walk the only reply they could elicit to their questions was a series of staccato snorts. On returning to the door, however, he turned and said, "Thanks for coming over, Sally. There is just one thing that you must not overlook."

"And what may that be, Major?"

"Why, the black hat of course. Good night, gentlemen."

CHAPTER 6

WHEN Percival Trout returned to his office on the campus on Friday, from his last class of the day, he found Cusani comfortably ensconced in his favorite chair, deeply immersed in Herrick's Introduction. He looked up as if annoyed at the interruption to his train of thought.

"Hello, Percy," he muttered, "I think I can get the hang on the invariable but the variable has me way up in a tree."

"Also many others," piped Trout gleefully. "Come on now, tell me all about it."

"Well, as I take it, invariable behavior is—"

"Not that stuff, you chump," squeaked Trout. "What about your murderer?"

"Oh that; we know who it is. It's just as I told you. We expect to pick him up anytime now."

"Well, who is it?"

"Just a cheap gun toter, as I told you. We heard from Hoover's boys in Washington. The finger-prints on the gun were Jim Romano's. He was acquitted at the time Judge Somers sent his twin brother up for a long stretch in that dope-ring case, last winter. It gives us a strong motive. Those twins were close to each other. They came from here and went to New York last year. Jim got off but Patsy took the rap. I think that some wise birds in the big town used them for a pair of punks."

"So what do you want now? You didn't come here to discuss neurology, did you?"

"Well, I'll tell you, Major. I didn't want to put all my eggs in one basket. What did you mean last night about the black hat?"

"Oh ho! So that's it, is it? What do you want to know about it?"

"I am going to come clean with you, Major. We know it is Redfield's. We also know that Redfield was in that room sometime during the afternoon yesterday. As a matter of fact, we have him down at headquarters now, but I can't get a damn thing out of him. He won't talk. He knows something, but he is scared, scared to death."

"Well, if you know Redfield was in the room," piped Trout, "you ought to know why he was there. If your only reason for thinking so is that you found his hat there, you may be shooting wide of the mark. Mind you, I don't say that you are wrong, but you can't be sure. You see, Sally, at sometime during the day some hats became mixed up. I don't yet know just when. Some one, sometime, may have changed hats with him."

"And given him the Judge's hat? Not very likely, Major."

"I did not say that he gave him the Judge's hat. I hope that you are not allowing yourself to be carried away by that performance in Dean Mather's office?" he said testily.

"Why sure; Redfield wore Judge Somers' hat into the Dean's office, didn't he?"

"Will you take your oath on that, Sally?"

"Well, I can swear to the fact that he did wear a black derby when he went in and that he wore no hat when he went out and that the Judge's hat was there in the room and when we all left there was no extra hat remaining. You can't laugh that off."

"I don't want to laugh off anything. I'll tell you one thing, however, and that is that we were damn careless in not making a complete check of all the hats before everybody left the Dean's office. It might have saved us a lot of time. Nevertheless, I can't see how you are going to prove the connection between Redfield and Judge Somers' hat."

"He was wearing it. Wasn't he?"

"I don't know. Was he?"

"Oh hell! Well he had it in his hands. You will admit that much anyway."

"Yes, I will grant that much. The hat was in the room."

"Well, if it was in the room, how did it get there if Redfield didn't wear it in? You tell me."

"Sally, me lad, I can give you several good reasons why that hat was in Mather's office. Prexy Davenport gave you an excellent one when he said that Somers may have left it there, but you wouldn't listen to him. However, that was not the hat that I was referring to last night. What about the hat up-stairs?"

"I told you about that one; it belongs to Redfield."

"I will admit that that is possible," said Trout. "But I do not consider the ownership of that hat the most important feature about it."

"What then, Major?"

"Among other things, the bullet holes and its position on the table. You didn't move it, did you? Do you know whether anyone else did? I don't believe that Judge Somers held that hat in front of him while he was struggling for that gun or at any other time. Do you? Of course you don't. All right then, listen to this. The bullet that went through that hat also passed through the Judge's body. Whether before or after, I do not know. Probably before on account of the large ragged hole it made. It naturally follows that that hat was in the room when he was killed."

"That's right, Major, and we know whose it is. It's Redfield's. He won't talk. It's his hat and he was in the room."

"Off you go again on a tangent. How about that gunman you had installed in the electric chair? What are you going to do with him? What makes you so sure that it was Redfield's hat anyway? Did he admit it?"

"No, he didn't; he won't say a word. But I am sure of it. It had his initials in it, 'J. R.' "

"I am inclined to agree with you that it is Redfield's hat, but not by pursuing the same reasoning as you. That gun-man you were talking about, what's his name? What were his—"

"Hell, Percy; you're right as usual. His initials are 'J. R.' too."

"Wasn't it you, my dear Sally, that said something about jumping to conclusions last night? No, my dear boy, I don't want to rub it in but I am afraid that in your anxiety, you are getting a bit careless. I am more than glad to set you straight if I can, but this case is not as simple as you seem to think. There is a lot of drift wood in the channel. Before we can sail our canoe without bumps, we have to clean all of that up. Some of it is below the surface, so let us be careful and proceed cautiously, lest we run against a snag."

"Sure, I'm just a wise-cracking sap, Major," said the chastened Cusani, "but let's skip it. What do you want me to do?"

"That's all right, Sally. None of us is perfect. I haven't the slightest idea yet, who killed my old friend. You may be right about Romano. We know he had a motive. On the other hand, Redfield may be the guilty one. We don't know *his* motive. Then again it may have been someone else."

"Has the coroner viewed the body?"

"Yeah. I went down to the morgue with him and the Chief. Doc. Mansfield was there and he went into a medical discussion with him. The bullet went straight through the body; practically horizontal, just clipping the heart and the aorta. He put it in plain English for our benefit. The verdict, of course, is murder and they are shipping the remains to New York today. The funeral will be held there Sunday. I'm sorry for that kid son of his. They say he's a swell guy. He couldn't have had anything to do with it, or could he?"

"Hell, Sally, there are 7,000 men at the University and more than 100,000 persons in the city. Any one of them, almost, could have killed the Judge. For instance where were you between 6:13 and 6:23 P.M. yesterday?"

"I was with the Chief in his office and that's my alibi. But, I guess you are right. I know what you mean. I think that we had better get down to that old Latin formula you were always quoting in France, 'Hic, Haec, Hoc,' or whatever it was. You know— 'Who, Why, When.' "

Trout threw himself back in his chair, laughing uproariously. "Sally, that's grand. A trifle free in the translation maybe, but perfect otherwise. You are a marvel. I never can tell what you are going to spring on me next."

There was a knock at the door and Dean Mather entered as Trout squeaked the invitation to come in.

"Sit down, Mather, sit down," he gasped. "Listen to Sally here. It's worth while, I assure you."

"Sorry, Percy, I am on my way to New York. Driving down with young Bob. I'll stay for the funeral on Sunday. I'll see you there. Is there anything I can do before I go?"

"Nothing, thanks, Bill. We will probably be back here Sunday night or Monday morning and if in the meantime anything should come up, we know how to get in touch with you."

When the Dean had gone, Cusani said, "The Dean and the Judge were pretty good friends, weren't they?"

"Yes, Sally, very good friends. Why?"

"Oh nothing. I was merely wondering. That's all. Could he have done it?"

Trout gazed speculatingly at his companion. Then he rose and commenced pacing up and down the room, his hands clasped behind his back, a deep frown on his ugly face.

"No, Sally," he said. "You are way off. Go along now and get Redfield to talk and pick up that Romano person. I have my own work to do."

When Cusani had gone, Trout sat huddled in his chair with a look of fear on his face, his mind filled with anxiety. He sat still for half an hour, then as if he had made up his mind to go through with some distasteful task, he leaped from his chair and rushed out of the room. In ten minutes he returned, his face ashen-pale, and taking a large calibre sporting rifle from under his coat, concealed it hurriedly in his closet.

CHAPTER 7

THAT EVENING Cusani sat at his desk at headquarters, making notes. Nothing seemed to please him, however, and he bunched them up and tossed them impatiently into the waste basket.

He was plainly worried. He knew that he could not hold Redfield much longer without possible censure. Romano was still eluding a wide-flung net. Trout was acting peculiarly. The whole case was at a standstill. He knew that those newspaper men had not been deceived for a minute and that he and the whole department were in for a hot panning in the New York and up-state journals. It might even result in state troopers being called in without protest on the part of the easy going Donovan. He weighed what evidence he had accumulated. Perhaps, after all it might be the smart thing to do if he gave Redfield a chance to prove his hunch. Redfield had seen Romano near the scene and perhaps he had something more tangible on which to go. Finn had also seen him . . . Finn? . . . After all why could not Finn have done it? Good old steady going

Pat, waiting for the time which was coming shortly when he could retire on a pension, But why? Certainly not for a few hundred dollars . . . If Finn was crooked and needed the money, he could get it in many other ways. But Cusani knew that Finn was comfortably off, having saved most of his salary over a long period of years and, besides that, Finn was given an alibi by Redfield. But Redfield's own alibi depended on Finn. Perhaps Redfield and Finn together . . . Well, maybe, but not likely; in fact most unlikely. However there was always a chance.

He lifted the telephone receiver and told the desk man if Finn was in the squad room to send him in. Presently Finn came in and eased himself into a chair with a smile on his weather-beaten face.

"I thought you'd be wanting to see me, Sally," he said.

"Yes, Pat, it's about Redfield. Your statement and his do not seem to jibe."

"Well my story is right, Sally. What I told you was straight."

"I'm not questioning that. Just when did you leave your post at the gate?"

"When the first fireworks went off. I followed the rules in the book what says that an officer, if he hears an unusual disturbance, kin leave his post to invest . . ."

"Yes, I know, Pat, I know the rules. What I want to know is if Redfield went into the campus too."

"He did, Sally."

"At the same time as you?"

"A few minutes ahead of me."

"Did you see him on the campus?"

"Well, I don't remember, Sally. There was a lot of guys there running around and yelling and shooting off fireworks."

"How well do you know this Redfield?"

"Oh, I know Johnny well. He's stationed at that gate regular. My beat is along there. I've known Johnny now for a couple of years. He's okay."

"Do you think that he could have shot the Judge?"

"Who? Johnny? No, Sally. Johnny ain't no killer. He's too soft."

"Do you know a fellow by the name of Jim Romano?"

"Romano?" Finn looked puzzled for a moment. Then his rugged features lighted up. "Romano," he repeated. "Say, Sally, that's the name of that guy."

"What guy?"

"Why, that wop what I was telling you about. You know, the one what came running out of the gate. The stemmer wid the cut face. Romano, that's his name."

"We are looking for him, Pat. Do you think that Redfield knows him?"

"I don't know, Sally. But Johnny ain't the kind to mix up with those hop heads. Johnny is classy and choosy."

"I suppose you know that we have Redfield locked up?"

"Yeah. But you are wrong there, Sally. Johnny ain't no killer."

"You said that before. But you can't be sure. As a matter of fact, you could have done it yourself."

"What, me?" Finn gasped. "You mean me kill the Judge?" He looked at the Sergeant aghast; his old face distorted as if in pain. Then searched Cusani's features as if to detect some latent joke. He laughed. "You sure have gone nuts, Sally. First, it's Redfield, then it's that hop head and now it's me. I know what you are trying to get at, though. You mean most any one could of done it. Sure they could. But I'm putting my dough on that Romano bird."

"Okay, Pat. That's all for now."

As Finn rose to go, he turned at the door and asked, "Where was that Dean Mather when it happened, Sally?"

"On the other side of the quadrangle. Why?"

"Nothing—I only wanted to know. So long."

Cusani sat silently pondering over the possibilities. Trout had deduced three visitors. Romano's prints on the gun; his strong motive, revenge; opportunity. Yes, it looked like Romano. But there was Redfield with the Judge's hat and a porous alibi. Motive? None that was known. Opportunity? None. For if Redfield had seen Romano leaving the section and, if the Judge had cut Romano's face, Redfield could not have killed the Judge, because if he had, the Judge could not have cut Romano's face . . . So . . . Who was the last man to see the Judge alive? Was it Romano? Mather? Bob? Who? Certainly not Redfield. He could not have gone up to the room after Romano had left. The time element made it impossible. Yes, Redfield might be of much more help outside.

He rose and went to the detention cells in the rear of the building where he opened the cell in which Redfield was incarcerated.

"All right, brother," he said. "You can go. But listen, don't do any fade-out to what the Jerries call 'wanderlust.' I'll be wanting to see you again tomorrow."

Redfield looked around suspiciously, then mumbled, "Want to see me down here?"

"No, I'll come up to your place in the afternoon. Perhaps you will talk to a friend of mine whom I'll bring along with me . . . No you don't need to worry . . . There'll be no strong arm stuff. You may trust me for that. Get a good night's rest and think over the advisability of giving me a little help. Good night now."

Redfield shuffled off with a muttered reply. Cusani smiled bitterly and shrugged his shoulders as he watched him depart. "There's something screwy about that bird. He reminds me of some one that I've seen a lot, but I can't place him. He is in this in some way. He's scared stiff and afraid to talk. Perhaps Percy Trout can get

something out of him. I can't see him as a killer though. Not deliberate anyway."

He went back to his office and sat at his desk with his elbows
on it and his head in his hands.

"Trout is afraid that I'll find out something about Mather. Why?
How could Mather have done it? And why again? There's something behind all this. Mather, Somers and Trout and that Tap Day
hocus pocus. Perhaps I am letting my imagination get the best of
me. Why bother with all that when Romano fits in so perfectly?
Better concentrate on getting him."

He looked at the clock, saw that it was after eight and picked
up his hat. As he was going out, he glanced at the telephone, hesitated a moment and called a number. The shrill voice of Percival
Trout answered almost at once.

"This is Sally, Major. I've just let Redfield go. Do you want to
tell me anything more?"

"No, not tonight. I am tired and I am going to bed early. Thanks
for calling me." Trout hung up.

"Now what in hell is biting him, I wonder?"

Cusani drove home slowly, meditating about the strange angles
the case was assuming and the unusual behavior of his friend
Trout. "I guess that's what that Herrick bird would call 'variable
behaviorism' all right," he decided, as he pulled up to the door of
his father's house.

Sally Cusani lived with his old parents in the house in which he
was born. The elder Cusani had been an emigrant who by diligence
and perseverance, having made a success in the wholesaling of
fruits, returned to Italy and brought back with him his boyhood
inamorata to the new home he had made for her in the land across
the seas. Salvatore was their only child and it is to his credit that
he was not spoiled by all the adoration his parents heaped upon
him. They never could talk enough about his "grand" friends. Once,
when in the line of duty, he was standing by the President of the
United States at the railroad station, the President turned to him
with a casual inquiry regarding the name of a veteran organization drawn up to meet him. The old couple who had witnessed the
scene, immediately elevated their son to a position of indispensable
confidant to His Excellency.

Sally had barely time to enter the front hallway, when his mother
ran out to meet him with affectionate greetings.

"Oh Sally, what do you think? Stuffed peppers! All ready and
waiting for you in the oven. The first ones this year! Your papa
got them special for you." She beamed on him proudly.

"Fine, Mama Mia, fine. How's papa?"

"Okay, Sally," called the old man from the sitting room. "How's
the boy?"

Old Cusani prided himself on his fluent Americanisms. He was a naturalized citizen and exceedingly grateful to his adopted country which had taken him to its bosom and repaid him well for his labors.

Sally sat down at the kitchen table to save his mother the extra steps, although a place had been set for him in the dining-room. The stuffed peppers with a decanter of red wine were soon disappearing with many a "Yum" and appreciative, if noisy, lip smacking to the delight of the old mother, when the sharp ring of the telephone bell made a strident interruption. He rose with a groan and answered it.

"Well?"

"Is that you, Sergeant?" it was Joe Blatchly calling.

"Yes, I'm eating my supper. What do you want?"

"Well, they've picked up Romano in Darien."

"So what?"

"They want for you to go down and bring him back, Sergeant."

"Is that so? Did you ever hear of variable and invariable behaviorism, Joe? Well it's always been invariable until now. Sally Cusani does all the work. It's going to be variable from now on. *You* go down and bring him back and I'll be seeing you in the morning. No, not tonight. I am tired and I am going to bed early. Thanks for calling." He hung up with a boyish grin at his mother.

"Education is a great thing, Mama," he said, "and I'm only beginning to learn now."

CHAPTER 8

MAMA CUSANI did pretty well for her son at breakfast; young scallions, chicken-liver-omelet with garlic embellishments and a huge pot of coffee. Later he went to his office reeking and eructing noisily and joyfully.

Joe Blatchly was seated at his desk. He shuffled to his feet on the Sergeant's entrance.

"Morning, Sergeant, I've got that hop-head Romano waiting for you. That was a helluva long ride last night," he added greatly aggrieved.

"The trouble with you, Joe," said Cusani smiling, "is lack of experience and I'm the one that's to blame for it. I have been hogging all the work and you and the other boys haven't had a show.

From now on I'll see to it that you have lots of opportunities. Did you search him?"

"Sure," replied the unhappy detective, "and he had plenty on him, too. He had ten packs of 'snow' in his clothes and we found about fifty more in the car."

"Okay, Joe, make out a charge for dope-running. I guess that we can make that stick. I don't want to see him now. Did he wear a hat?"

"Yeah. A black derby."

"Bring it in, I want to see it."

When Blatchly returned with the hat, Cusani examined it carefully. It was an ordinary black derby of fair quality, practically brand new, with a local haberdasher's label and the initials "J. R." perforated in the sweat-band.

"I want you to trace this hat, Joe, and see whether it is his or not."

Blatchly smiled and with a superior air, said, "You want to know whether it's his or not? Say, Sargeant, you didn't miss those letters did you? 'J. R.' 'Jim Romano' you know."

"Thanks, Joe. I must say that's damn smart of you. 'J. R.' 'Jim Romano.' Well, well— Now, you big stiff, beat it and do as I told you or I'll kick your fat fanny across the Green."

After Blatchly had gone Sally sat at his desk. For an hour he was busy with routine reports. Afterwards he sat for a while in deep thought. Finally he drew the telephone towards him and gave a number. Trout's voice answered.

"Look here, Major," he said, "I need your help and I need it badly. I want to come up to see you, to talk that hat business over. It's Saturday and you haven't any classes today. How about it?"

"Well all right. Come up if you want to," sighed Trout hopelessly.

"There's something biting the old boy and I think I can put my finger on it," murmured Sally as he hung up the receiver.

A few minutes later, Cusani was seated in Trout's office on the campus.

"I find that I am neglecting my work," Trout said peevishly, "with all this extraneous activity and I have about decided to drop this case. However I could not resist your plea to talk hats with you. Go ahead."

"All right, hats it is. I've made a list of all the hats we know about that have entered the case so far. I have it here. I'm taking only the black derbies into consideration. First, and probably most important, is the one which we found upstairs in the room where the Judge's body was lying. It had a big, ragged hole in it on each side as if a spent bullet had passed through it. Inside was the mark of a local clothier and also the initials 'J. R.' stuck on in gilt paper letters. I think we can safely assume that it belongs to either John Redfield or to Jim Romano. Right so far, Major?"

"Yes, I think we may accept that as a fact."

"Whose hat it is I may be able to verify today. I believe it is Redfield's. By the way, Major, we picked up Romano last night. He was wearing a black derby; almost new. If he bought it before Thursday afternoon, that would tie the one with the holes in it to Redfield."

"Yes. It probably would," said Trout spiritlessly.

Cusani glanced at him curiously, but went on with his summary. "I'm going to get this hat business straightened out first and see where it leads us. The next hat in order of importance would seem to be the Judge's. That hat was found downstairs in the Dean's office. It had Judge Somers' name spelled out in full and there can be no doubt of ownership. The question, therefore, arises, how did it get there? Redfield had it in his hands and repudiated it. That hat was hot. He went out bareheaded, but earlier when he was outside and I was talking to him, *he was wearing a black derby hat!*

"The question arises—why do questions always 'arise,' Major? You always hear of lawyers 'putting' the question. Don't they ever stay 'put'? Do they always have to 'arise'? Well, anyway, the question presents itself, what hat was Redfield wearing? Was he wearing Judge Somers' hat and became panicky when the conversation turned to hats during my questioning of young Somers? Or was he wearing another hat entirely? Pure reason, as our French colleague, Captain Denis in Paris, was always saying, would certainly and unqualifyingly tell us that he was wearing the Judge's hat."

"You forgot 'beyond peradventure of any doubt' or 'indubitably,' Sally," piped up Trout, who was beginning to take more interest in the proceedings. "I also like that new word of yours. 'Unqualifyingly' has a smack of ruthlessesss about it. But, go on, go on."

Cusani gave him one of his quizzical smiles and went on, "I therefore know that Redfield was lying to us. President Davenport suggested that Judge Somers left his hat in the Dean's office and went upstairs bareheaded. That theory is exploded by the fact that young Somers saw his father at the window with his hat on and again by the fact that when we left the Dean's office, there was no surplus of hat. It follows therefore that Redfield took the hat in exchange for his. Why? I'll tell you why and I have thought this out only this moment, because while he was up there his own hat was shot through and so badly damaged that he didn't dare to be seen in it for fear of drawing attention to himself. He therefore took the Judge's hat. Now you said yourself that the same bullet that killed the Judge also punctured that hat. I have proved that Redfield was in the room when that bullet was fired. Therefore *John Redfield murdered Judge Somers.*"

"Great, Sally, great! But again you forgot something. How about 'ergo' and 'Q.E.D.' No, Sally, I don't agree. You started out all right but you shunted yourself off on a side-track. But go on. Let's hear the rest of it."

"Well, I guess that's about all there is," said the Sergeant dejectedly.

"Nonsense," snorted Trout, "you have an almost Homeric catalogue of hats there in your hand. Get on with it."

"All right. The next black derby was the one that Gregory wore. Gregory was one of the first to find the body. He and young Somers according to their story, reached the room almost at the same time; Somers first and he immediately after. They both declare that neither entered the room. That is probably correct, as Dean Mather could not have been more than a minute behind. Young Somers wore no hat. The next one is Dean Mather's. But as he was out of the section when the shot was fired and was wearing his own hat when he left for New York, I can't fit that one in as part of the picture. He was the first one to go into the room after the killing as far as we know, but I can't see that that has anything to do with the hat question, and that, after all is the only matter under discussion at present."

He looked questioningly at Trout who frowned and said, "Yes, that's right. Let's stick to our hats. Go on."

"Well, the next black derby is Chief Donovan's. I was with the Chief when the crime was committed or at least during the time we figured out it must have been committed, that is between 6:20 and 6:23 and I also was with him when he left the section, so I can't see how his hat can have any bearing on the matter. Then the last black derby is President Davenport's which I saw him wearing when he left us in Dean Mather's office. That's all. You wore that gray Homburg on the rack over there, Blatchly wore a brown soft Fedora, Doc. Mansfield had on a new spring model, very chaste. None of the men from headquarters had black derbies. They wore uniform caps, while yours truly was bedecked with this fawn-colored snapper which my hatter assures me is the last word from the stylists in Danbury. Thus, ergo (by request), I think that brother Redfield is the leading candidate for the hot seat."

He looked at Trout triumphantly, "Tie a can to that if you're able."

"Look here, Sally," said Trout seriously. "Are you sure of your data? And when I say 'data' I mean data—the known facts. No hypotheses, no deductions, no inferences, no hear-say, no guessing, but the plain cold facts as you saw them. Now repeat what you saw. Give me the names again of every one who wore a black derby hat when he left the section Thursday evening. Think carefully," he cautioned. "Try to picture each man in your mind's eye."

Trout's seriousness was infectious and Cusani glanced 'over his list before he replied.

"All right. I will take them in order of their departure. The first that I saw leave was Chief Donovan. The next was Gregory. Then came Redfield— Hold on though. He wasn't wearing a hat then. After him was President Davenport and then Dean Mather. That I will swear to. I can see each man with his hat on his head. That is absolutely correct, Major."

"If you have made a mistake, you are going to make an ass of me, but I know from experience, that when it comes to factual observation, you seldom err. All right I'm banking on you. Come on," he said, rising and reaching for his hat. He led the astonished Sergeant to his parked car. Trout took the wheel and drove up to a stately old house on a broad street shaded with rows of ancient elms.

"Follow me," he said as he started across the side-walk.

They were admitted by an elderly, dignified negro who smiled broadly as he recognized Trout.

"Yas, Perfesser Trout, sah. De Doctor am in de liberry. Ah will have de pleasure to 'nounce you."

He led them to a book-lined room where President Davenport rose to greet them cordially.

"Ah, Dr. Trout, I am delighted to see you and this gentleman with you is—?"

"Sergeant Cusani of the city police, Dr. Davenport."

"Of course, Sergeant. Pardon me for not recognizing you at once, but I am having some slight difficulty with my eyes. Pray be seated, gentlemen. I presume that you have come to tell me the results of your investigations in the shocking death of my good friend."

"I am afraid, Dr. Davenport, that we have not made much progress there yet. But there is one thing in which you may be able to set us right."

"Anything that I can do for you, certainly, Dr. Trout, certainly."

"Do you possess a black derby hat?" asked Trout intently.

"A black derby hat?" queried the amazed Davenport. "Oh I see, a bowler. Why yes, I am rather partial to a bowler and wear one usually on all informal occasions. I may have several. Adams will know. Why do you ask?"

"We are trying to clear up a point in our investigations and in the process of elimination it becomes necessary to identify all the hats that were in Dean Mather's office on Thursday," explained Trout.

"Ah yes. I see. I recall now there was some question about how Judge Somers' hat could have been in that room and I gave what I thought was the obvious solution. If I remember correctly, that solution did not meet with favor. Has a better suggestion been advanced since them.

"No, Dr. Davenport, there has not," answered Trout with a smile. "And it is for that reason we are here. Do you recall what hat you were wearing yourself, Thursday afternoon?"

Davenport screwed up his myopic eyes and pressed a button saying, "Just a moment, Doctor, I will ask Adams. He may remember."

The old negro appeared promptly.

"Adams, do you recall what hat I wore Thursday afternoon?"

After a few moments of puzzled cogitation, Adams replied, "I cain't say, Doctor, I cain't say for sure. No, sah, I must apologize for that lapse of memory."

"Would you let me see your hats, Dr. Davenport?"

"Certainly. Adams, will you bring in my hats for Dr. Trout?"

"The black derbies, only, Adams," amended Trout.

Adams returned and placed three hats on the table with a flourish of showmanship worthy of a Barnum.

Trout examined them eagerly. They all bore the mark of a hatter on Ludgate Hill, London. He rose without showing the disappointment he felt. Thanked Davenport and took his departure followed by the silent Cusani.

On the side-walk he stopped and deliberated. He looked at Cusani thoughtfully, and muttered, "There's something wrong here. I can't have reasoned this out in any other way and I used only pure ratiocination. I know I must be right, but there is a hitch somewhere. I wonder—" He stopped short and laughed. "Why of course that's it. It's all my own fault. It only goes to show that a slight error will make one doubt even pure reasoning which can never be wrong. Come on, Sally." So saying, he led the way back to the house.

When Adams answered the bell, Trout said, "Sorry to trouble you again, Adams, but there is another question which I meant to ask you. Are there any other black derbies in the house besides those of the Doctor's?"

"Yas, there is. I did not think that you desired to view it, sah. It is not of the lofty saturnial puffection of our wardrobe. It is reclining in the hall cabinet. I will repossess it if you so desire."

"Please do so, Adams," smiled Trout.

Trout examined the hat eagerly after Adams had presented it to him with a wide flourish. He gave a grunt of satisfaction and handed it to Cusani as he said, "Take a good look at this now. Then give it back to Adams who will be glad to take good care of it for us."

They drove back to Trout's room, the Major with a canary-stuffed expression and smirk, and the Sergeant in stupefied amazement. Not until they were seated in their customary places, did either one break the silence and then Cusani exploded his pent-up emotions.

"Well I'll be a—never mind, but who in hell would have thought of it?"

"Well, I did for one," pointed out the Major.

"I'll be doubly damned. His own son!"

"Certainly young Robert Somers' name was in that hat and there is no reason why we should doubt his ownership. That he had anything to do with killing his father, however, is an entirely different matter and has nothing to do with the subject under discussion, which, if I recall correctly, was to be confined to one item only and that was hats. I suppose you want to know how young Somers' hat got into Prexy's house and how I knew that we would find it there."

"That's the ticket, Butch. Tell me."

"In a few minutes. It's time for lunch. Will you honor me with your company and we can continue the hat saga afterwards or—"

"Cripes, Percy, I had no idea that it was so late. No. I'll tell you what we'll do. Mama told me this morning that she was making same mushroom sauce and I could have some spaghetti with it for lunch today. You come along with me. She'd be tickled pink to see you again; so would the old man. She says that you are the only one who will talk wop with her. The old man will only talk American and I guess my Italian is as bad as my English. I'll call her up now and tell her we are coming. We can stop at headquarters on our way over."

CHAPTER 9

TROUT AND CUSANI were smoking their cigarettes after disposing of approximately two hundred yards of spaghetti, or as Sally said with a smile, "a derby hat full," when the Major remarked casually, "I think that I will go to New York tonight. There are some people I want to see and I will stay over for Judge Somers' funeral. You are getting along all right. I agree that in this case, the best thing to do is to eliminate one puzzle at a time. This hat problem should be cleared up first. I think that you will agree with me when I say that as soon as we have that straightened out, we can proceed with more intelligence. The matter of the Judge's ring, I have already solved and will explain later; also the chip of brick, although some things about that are not entirely clear. Your two suspects, Redfield and the gangster, may yield something. I will leave them to you until I get back; but if I were you, I would not let Redfield out of my sight a minute."

"I've put a tail on him. He can't get away, Major."

"Now about those hats—Oh by the way. What report did you get on the one that Romano was wearing? It was his own, wasn't it?"

"Yeah, it was, and that dumb cluck, Blatchly, is still laughing at me. I saw him posing for the *New York Express* photographer as 'The Man Who Caught Romano.' Amos down in Darien, will get a big kick out of that."

"All right then, that, I think, straightens out everything except the position of the hat on the table."

"Maybe it does to you, Major and maybe I'm pretty thick, but I'll be damned if I can see how anything is straightened out at all. Tell me."

"Perhaps I was not quite fair to you, Sally. You did not know everything I knew, but on the other hand, there were some things you knew that I did not. Some of this is conjecture, some of it is pure reasoning, but there are enough data mixed in to make it stick together. Here it is. When the Judge went upstairs, he left his hat in Dean Mather's office. Please don't interrupt; you may ask all the questions you wish when I am through. It was late in the day and cool when he stood by the open window. He looked around the room and found his son's hat which he put on. He had at least two visitors; Redfield and Romano. I think that we are safe in saying that the hat which was left in the room, was Redfield's and the revolver was Romano's. Now, as Redfield was wearing a black derby hat *after* his call on the Judge and had left his own upstairs, it follows that he brought a strange hat into the Dean's office. A hat, which he probably exchanged for his own, upstairs. Now as he did not carry it out of the Dean's office himself, he must have left it there and some one else carried it out. The question is therefore, who was it that came into the office bare-headed and left with a hat on? The answer is—President Davenport, who, as you may have noticed, is not only absent-minded, but near-sighted.

"When Mather telephoned him the news of the Judge's death, he said that he was in his office on the quadrangle over by the chapel. I was playing the organ and he rushed over and dragged me into this mess. He was quite perturbed; in fact had not stopped to put on his hat. You did not see him when he came into the Dean's office; you were upstairs. I did not see him as he went out. He was talking to Mather while I was trying to get some line on the case, by listening in on your telephone talk with Donovan. I had my back turned to him. As soon as you made out that hat inventory, this morning, I knew that President Davenport had carried out the missing hat. That was simple, but it had me puzzled.

"Now you will want to know how the hats got mixed up in the Dean's office. I am confident Redfield was not aware of the fact that

the hat he was wearing was not his own until the talk began to center around the hat left upstairs. It bothered him. He looked at the
hat he was holding. To his horror, he saw that it was not his. He decided to pass it on to some one else. Exchange it at once—get it off
his hands. He therefore laid it down and picked up the nearest one.
Imagine his consternation, when talking to your man Blatchly, he
looked at the lining, and found himself with the Judge's hat in his
hands. The most incriminating evidence of all! He became panic-
stricken and tried to run away. I think that straightens out all the
hats."

"Thanks, Major. That's clear now. I suppose that that poor tripe,
Redfield, is wondering what we think and how much we suspect
him. I'll bet that's why I can't get him to talk. He's afraid to open
his mouth for fear that he'll make another blob. I made a date to see
him again this afternoon and had hoped that you would come along.
I anticipated that you might get him to talk. He seems to be scared
of cops. Anyway he will have a lot of explaining to do about why his
hat was in the same room with Judge Somers' body. Will you come
with me? It would help a lot. I got the impression, when I talked
with him, that he wanted to tell me something but did not dare to. If
you were there with me, he might lose his fear. He has a complex,
that all the police want to do is to beat up prisoners, that no witness
is safe from third degree stuff. With you there, he'd have more confidence. The poor punk knows that you wouldn't stand for any rough
stuff, therefore he might open up to you."

"I don't know that it will be any use," said Trout, "but I will go
with you. Perhaps it will set my mind at rest on another matter,"
he added wearily.

Redfield occupied rooms in a good section of the city. The fine
comfortable-looking house caused Trout to raise his eye-brows and
emit a puzzled grunt as they ascended the front steps. They were admitted by an unusually good-looking young woman, well dressed and
self-assured. She scrutinized Cusani for a moment and glanced inquiringly at Trout, then addressing herself to the Sergeant said,
"You are Detective Cusani, aren't you?"

"Yes, mam," answered Sally, "and this gentleman is Professor
Trout of the University.".

"Yes," she said with a pleasant nod to the bowing Percival, "we
all have heard of Dr. Trout. Mr. Redfield is expecting you, Mr.
Cusani, but before I show you to his rooms, I'd like to talk with you
both. Please come into the living room with me."

Without waiting for a reply, she led them through a door opening
into the hall.

When they had entered she closed the door carefully and faced
them with a challenge in her shrewd, black eyes.

"Please sit down, gentlemen," she said. "What I am going to tell

you, I believe, is of the greatest importance. I am Elsie Fernaud
My mother owns this house. We run a boarding-house. My mothe
is not in good health, so most of the responsibility falls to me. Ou
place is one of the best in town, which I believe can be verified. Yo
may therefore think it strange that a man in Mr. Redfield's positio
can afford to occupy our best suite of rooms, but the explanation i
simple. Mr. Redfield has a private income which is paid to him onl
if and when he can prove that he is gainfully employed to his guard
ian monthly."

As Cusani was about to interrupt, she said quickly, "Please le
me finish. You don't know Johnny Redfield. I do. He has lived her
for nearly three years. He has never been trained to do anythin
useful. He has no aspirations to greatness. He is happy and conten
as he is. He has never had a living relative as long as he can remem
ber. When he came to us practically without a friend, I was sorr
for him. Such a big handsome fellow, with such friendly blue Iris
eyes, but so utterly and futilely helpless. He was only a boy. He i
only twenty-three now. I am three years older. I know somethin
of life. I've had to make my own way since my father died, seve
years ago. Johnny used to come to me for advice and soon becam
dependent on me. When this horrible thing happened and he becam
involved in it, he came to me and told me everything. I comforte
him. I advised him to go to the police and to make a clean breast o
the whole matter. That he has now promised to do, but he wanted m
to see you first and explain the situation.

"He has an overwhelming fear of third-degree methods. I dis
agree with him. I'm sure you'd treat him fair. Nevertheless,
promised him I would remain in the room with you while you wer
questioning him. Before we go, however, I want to tell you on
thing. If you believe for one moment that Johnny Redfield had any
thing to do with the murder of Judge Somers, get it out of you
minds at once. I know him so well that it is ridiculous to even con
sider it."

As she finished speaking, Cusani said, "I don't know whether o
not it would be all right to have you there, Miss. It's most irreg
ular."

"If I am to be excluded, he won't say anything; so you'd bette
make up your mind right away."

Trout intervened hastily as he saw an angry flush appearing o
his companion's face and piped out with a broad smile, "Why o
course, Sergeant. That's perfectly regular. Redfield is entitled to a
attorney and Miss Fernaud is merely acting in that capacity in thi
particular case."

Elsie stood stiffly silent until Cusani shrugged his shoulders an
nodded his acquiescence. Then she led them to a door farther dow
the hall and rapped lightly.

CHAPTER· 10

THE ROOM INTO which Elsie ushered Trout and Cusani was well furnished, several comfortable chairs, a walnut table, an upholstered divan. The floor rug was Oriental. A bookcase stood against one wall, etchings decorated the others. The only thing lacking was individuality. It was as if one were gazing into the show window of a better class furniture store. There was nothing there that reflected personality. This struck Trout at once. He smiled as he reflected, that after all, Redfield's character was strikingly mirrored for he was totally lacking in personality.

Redfield rose to his feet as they entered, a sheepish look on his almost too handsome face. His high complexion and blue eyes, his short straight nose and well-formed brow were not spoiled by the weak lower lip. He glanced furtively toward Elsie who smiled and gave him a reassuring nod.

"Everything is all right, Johnny," she murmured. Then she turned to the others and said, "Please make yourselves comfortable, gentlemen. There are cigarettes over there on the smoking stand and some bottled beer on the ice, if you care for it. Mr. Redfield is quite ready to answer any questions you may wish to ask him that may help to clear up this frightful affair."

Choosing a chair next to Redfield, she lighted a cigarette and said tauntingly, "Now you may proceed with the inquisition, Mr. Cusani."

"I am sorry, Miss Fernaud," he said quietly, "that you are taking such an attitude. I am only trying to straighten out some snarls in a cowardly killing and I was looking to you for co-operation. There will be no inquisition as you seem to fear, but a fair and honest effort to get at the truth."

Elsie looked at him, not a whit abashed, but with a trace of respect she had not shown hitherto, and said, "I'm sorry that you should have so misunderstood me. I did not intend to use the term in its cruel or inhuman sense, but merely as applied to any questioning. Please go on."

Meanwhile Trout was watching Redfield, trying hard to conceal the contempt he felt for him. He was attempting to classify him so that he could file him away in what he called his "mental cabinet" in which were pigeon-holed many subjects under his own descriptive and distinctive names.

"He is either a 'prat' or a 'gomph,'" he decided. Elsie he had already filed away as a "vim," which was a very high rating.

Cusani turned to Redfield. "I want to assure you that if you are innocent of crime, you have nothing to fear from me. Are you ready to tell us what you were doing Thursday afternoon up to the time that I gave you permission to go from Dean Mather's office?"

Redfield turned timorously toward Elsie who nodded reassuringly. "All right, Sergeant," he said. "I took my post at the east portal where I was joined by officer Finn at three o'clock. About that time, Judge Somers came along and I asked him if I could see him about an important matter. He replied that he had an appointment with the Dean, but could give me a few minutes afterwards and that he would be in his son's room, over the Dean's office around six. At six I went up to see him and stayed only three or four minutes. I left in a hurry and somehow picked up the wrong hat. I then went to see another man. I got back to my post a few minutes before Dean Mather called me. I guess that's all."

"That's not all and you know it!" barked out Cusani. "You'll have to do a lot more explaining before I am satisfied."

Redfield turned to Elsie. "I told you so," he said. "They don't believe me and now they'll give me the needles."

"No Johnny, they won't. Don't worry," she said soothingly, then turning to Cusani, she demanded, "What more do you want to know?"

"Why, the whole story is ridiculous. Why should a man like Judge Somers make an appointment with a campus cop?"

"Why not?" countered the girl.

"All right; he did then. What was the appointment for? What did he want? Who was the man he went to see afterwards?"

"That is all a private matter and unless Mr. Redfield wishes to tell you, I don't see that you have any right to know about it."

"Look here, Miss," exclaimed the indignant Sergeant. "Are you trying to give me a tossing? Private affairs and murder don't mix. What have you got to do with it anyway? Redfield is old enough and big enough to take care of himself. So let him do his own explaining and you keep out of it."

"Very well. I will keep out of it, Mr. Cusani. Mr. Redfield and I will therefore bid you good-by."

Trout saw that it was time for him to interfere if the situation was to be saved from becoming a ridiculous farce. With a beaming smile he addressed himself to the angry girl.

"My dear young lady there is nothing more admirable than loyalty. I fully appreciate what you are doing for our young friend and I must also thank you for what you have done so far for us. I am sure that Sergeant Cusani is grateful for the information which you and Mr. Redfield have given us. I am afraid, however, that in your zeal to protect your friend's undobuted prerogatives, you may have mistaken our mission here. We came not to make any accusations. I don't believe for a moment that Redfield had any hand in killing Judge Somers. I am sure that he did not. But there is something else to be explained that involves him so deeply, that if I were in his shoes, I too, would be as disturbed as he appears to be."

Trout's three listeners gazed at him with varied emotions; Cusani doubtfully, the girl suspiciously and Redfield fearfully. After a pause, pregnant with tension, he continued almost casually, "And now, Redfield, perhaps you will tell us why you stole that money from Judge Somers."

"It's a lie! I didn't steal it. He gave it to me."

"Thank you, Redfield. That was what we wanted to know," said Trout with a satisfied smile.

Elsie sprang to her feet, her fists clenched, her trim boyish figure vibrant with passion as she arrayed herself in front of Redfield, as if to protect him from any further attack.

"Shame, Dr. Trout, shame. You, a man of experience, to take a mean advantage of a mere boy. That was a shabby trick."

"Well, I admit I'm not proud of it and I won't even quote the obvious excuse in justification, but there is no need for dramatics. Please sit down and listen to me."

He paused as he lighted a fresh cigarette. As he shook out the match, he continued, "I am going to be perfectly frank with you. I expect you and Redfield to reciprocate. We came here this afternoon in a spirit of helpfulness. We knew that Redfield had been to see Judge Somers. We knew that the Judge had given him the money. We also believed that the money had been given to him freely. What we do not know and what I think you should suggest to your friend to tell us, is why the money was given to him and what his connection is with Judge Somers. If it has no bearing on the murder, you may rest assured that we will hold it in strict confidence. Is that fair, or not?"

Elsie looked at Redfield, but he shook his head stubbornly.

"Perhaps it would be best, Johnny," she said. "I think the Doctor is right. Of course I don't know all the details myself, so I can't be sure. I think that they want to be fair."

Redfield sat several minutes in moody silence as the others waited for his reply.

Finally he addressed Trout, "Before I say anything, I want to know how much Dean Mather has told you about me."

"Nothing at all," answered Trout puzzled.

Redfield hesitated, then turned to Cusani. "Will you promise me the cops won't beat me up?" he asked with trepidation.

"Don't worry about that, I give you my word."

"All right, then. I was two months back in my payments on my car and the finance company was going to snatch it. They gave me until half past six on Thursday to get the dough. I asked the Judge to lend it to me. He said, 'Sure,' and took it out of his wallet and handed it to me. I ran out in a hurry and grabbed the wrong hat and met the finance man and paid him. That's why I was away from the portal so long. I came through the west portal. Jimmy Murray, the guard, saw me coming in. You can ask him. If you want to see the receipt from the finance company, I can show you that too. I got back just as Dean Mather came out and called me. I guess that's all and I hope you are satisfied now."

"Thank you, Redfield," interposed Trout quickly, in order to fore-stall Cusani who was about to break in. "I think that covers practically all we want to know. You were gone from your post from six o'clock to almost six thirty. Is that right?"

"Yes, sir."

"Did you see any one or anything unusual when you returned, before Dean Mather called you."

"No, sir. I was in a hurry to get back. I didn't see anybody but Finn and that 'Jimmy the wop.' "

"I wish that you had told us all that before, Redfield. It would have saved us time and trouble. Perhaps you may care to tell me what Dean Mather knows?"

"No I won't," replied Redfield sullenly. "If he didn't say anything, I don't see why I should."

"We will forget that then. If Mather wants to tell me, he will. You might tell us instead how Judge Somers came to lend you the money."

"I told you. Because I needed it."

"Yes, I know. But that isn't all. Judge Somers is not the kind of a man to hand out a large sum of money to any one who asks for it. Come, Redfield, better tell us all about it."

"There's nothing more to tell. I asked him for it and he let me have it."

And with that they had to be content, for not another word of explanation would he vouchsafe.

Elsie accompanied them to the door and as they were making their departure, smiled charmingly at Cusani and said, "I'm sorry, Mr. Cusani, for my stupidity in hindering you in your duty and I apologize. Please forgive me."

The embarrassed Sally mumbled some commonplace and the two investigators drove off.

CHAPTER 11

"**I**F I EVER FELT like giving any one a paste on the puss, it was today," said Cusani when they had returned to Trout's rooms.

"Can you imagine that big boob hiding behind that swell dame's skirts? I'd like to have pushed his face in for him. I think the big bum is a blackmailer if nothing worse. When it all comes out, you'll see that he had something on the Judge and has been bleeding him for a long time. We know that he has been spending more than his salary. That bunk he told Miss Fernaud about an income is a lot of hooey. You notice he didn't say anything to us about it. You bet he didn't. He knew damn well we could check up on it too easy. So he faked that story about borrowing the money from the Judge. He must have thought we were a couple of prize saps to swallow it. She believed him too, because I think that she is a square-shooter and if she thought that there was anything crooked going on, she'd give him the gate. What do you think, Percy?"

"I think you're right about the girl, Sally. She's straight. But you're not entirely correct about Redfield. I believe everything that he told us, but he did not tell us everything that he could. Cast out of your mind at once any idea that Somers was permitting any one to blackmail him. He gave Redfield the money freely all right. Why, I don't know just now, but I will make it my business to find out. As to Redfield, he isn't even a boob, he is a 'prat.'"

"What in hell is a 'prat'?" exclaimed the astonished Sergeant.

"I don't think that I could make you understand, Sally, but it is a cross between a fourmart and a siphonophore."

"Thanks for the explanation. It makes it as clear as mud, but somehow, it seems to fit him all right." Cusani grinned and then asked, "I wonder what he meant when he asked you if Dean Mather had told you anything."

"I haven't the slightest idea," answered Trout and added bursquely, "I have a lot of things to do, if I want to get off to New York this evening and, if there is nothing else, you will have to excuse me now."

Sally Cusani drove slowly to his office, turning over in his mind the incidents of the afternoon and the abrupt congé he had received at Trout's hands. He found Blatchly fast asleep at his desk and relieved his own feelings by tipping him out of the chair.

"Jeese, Sergeant," whined the outraged Joe. "If you had to drive way down to Darien and capture a prisoner like you made me do, you'd want a little rest, too. This is a helluva job, all work and no-body gives you no credick. Did you grab your killer yet?"

"No, not yet, Joe. Perhaps instead of sleeping on the job when you ought to be working, you might put that massive brain of yours into action and earn some of the money that the taxpayers are giving you."

"Ah, Sarge, what's the use of chasing all over for the killer when I brought him in myself last night?"

"Sez you."

"Yeah and I ain't the only one that sez it. Chief Donovan and that smart guy from the New York paper think so, too. You're wasting your time, Sarge. Romano is hot and I can get him to spill the stuff, if the Chief will let me. That New York guy told me some new ones and they are the goods."

"Lay off that line, Joe. Don't let me hear any more about it. I have a lot of things to do," he added with a smile, "and if there's nothing else, you will have to excuse me now."

"Well, ain't you going to talk to Romano at all?"

"He can wait a little while longer. It will do him good. Stick around and bring him in here in a half an hour. Now get out."

"Cripes, Sergeant, have a heart. I was just going home to my supper."

"Your supper can wait, too. It will do you good."

Blatchly went out grumbling as Cusani seated himself at his desk and concentrated on the problem. As far as the murder was concerned, the interview with Redfield had been a wash-out. They were no further advanced than before. He went over the events of the afternoon again. That girl certainly was swell. He could not get her out of his mind. The way she stood up to him and protected that poor sap. How sweetly she apologized when Percy had taken her to task.

"Fernaud?" The name was familiar. "Of course! She must be the daughter of Jules Fernaud, a French-Canadian building contractor who had had some success for a time and died a few years ago. Elsie Fernaud, eh? Gee—I don't suppose that she would look twice at a cop. But still—well I'd better forget it now and do something to earn my pay as I told Joe."

He drew out some note paper and jotted down some memoranda. He made a list of all, who in any way, could come under suspicion.

Redfield—Was in the room. Had opportunity. Admits getting the money. Is holding something back.

Romano—Was recognized by Finn near the scene. Gun and bullet probably his. Had grudge. Motive. Finger-prints.

Bob Somers—Had access to room. First to see body. Possible but unlikely.

Gregory—Not likely unless in cahoots with Bob. Could have, but

Mather was too close on their heels.

Mather—Was not in the vicinity, had gone across the campus, but ... and it dawned on him suddenly how Mather could have done it. That was why Trout was so perturbed every time Mather's name was brought up.

"He suspected him from the first," he mused. "An explorer, probably a dead shot with a rifle. Not more than two hundred yards across the campus. A cinch for him. But how about the bullet? That's not so easy. Let me think now. Where could that have gone? It may have ricocheted, but where? Wow! I've got it. That chip of brick from the fire-place. That's it. The fire-place is in line with the window. But the bullet? Let's see—He was the first in the room. He might have picked it up. I must ask Somers and Gregory. Then Redfield mentioned his name, too. But why? Why? If I could find a motive, I could get a search warrant and go through his rooms. I wonder how much Percy has got on him. I'll bet it's plenty or he wouldn't be so worried. If anybody knows the motive, *he* would. Would he double-cross me and warn him? I wonder. No question about that. That's what he was preparing for last night. But I can't arrest him on what I think. I haven't a bit of proof. That's been the trouble with this case from the start. Plenty of clues but no proof. I've got to talk to Percy no matter how he feels about it. This is a murder case and if he knows anything, he will have to come clean."

He reached for the telephone and called Trout. "Can you give me a few minutes on something important, Major?"

"No."

"But this is of vital importance."

"I don't give a damn. I'm just leaving for New York and haven't a minute to spare."

"It's about Dean Mather," Cusani whispered.

There was a slight pause before Trout answered, "What about him?"

"Do you know when he is coming back?"

"No. Why?"

"Because I want to see him."

"Why?"

"Please be reasonable, Major. You suspect him yourself. Now will you see me if I come up?"

"You're crazy, and I warn you right now to be careful what you do or say. Stick to your gun-man and keep out of things you don't understand. I'll be back Monday, maybe tomorrow night, and I will try to put you on the right track. In the meantime don't make a fool of yourself." Trout hung up as Blatchly came in with Romano in tow.

Cusani waved them to chairs. He seemed worried. "I wish I could be sure," he muttered. "Percy didn't deny a thing. What can I do?

I can't order a man like Dean Mather to be pulled in on mere suspicion. I can't stop Trout from warning him."

An admonitory cough from the impatient Blatchly recalled him to the more immediate work before him. He looked up and saw facing him a young Italian, a typical gangster. One of those dark, vicious rats, spewed from the slimy sewer of iniquitous abomination, that had cast a curtain of obloquy on the millions of decent, hard-working citizens of Italian extraction.

Cusani forced himself into a state of imperturbable composure as he scrutinized the prisoner. He saw a young man, scarcely out of his teens with a hard face and thin snarling lips, greasy hair, cold black eyes. He was dressed in pseudo-collegiate clothes. Sally had handled many of his kind before. They all had the same vulnerability; a horror of ridicule and a warped pride in their criminality. He smiled sardonically and said, "So you are Jim Romano? Well, well. I know all about you and I haven't stopped laughing yet. You're the little mama's boy that burst out crying when he was pinched in New York. You and that twin brother of yours, a couple of small-time punks, went down to the big city thinking that you were big shots, and were taken over the jumps by the wise guys. Now they tell me you're running snow for some other smart bird who is making a sucker of you again. My God, you certainly are the original come-on; Mr. Hicks from Hicksville. Well, what have you got to say for yourself?"

Romano swallowed hard, but remained silent. Sally laughed as he went on, "Afriad to talk, eh? Scared of some gorilla who might slap you on the wrist? Well I can't blame you for that and I'm sorry for you, too. Just a poor misguided kid. You don't belong here. I think that I'll send you to the juvenile court with the apple snatchers and put you in charge of the matron."

Romano flushed with suppressed anger, but kept his mouth closed tightly.

"So you can't take it, eh?" taunted Cusani. "You haven't got a come-back. Just a cheap punk as I thought. Afriad to say anything because you might give yourself away? Now, all the big shots are willing to talk. They know how to say enough without committing themselves, but you little pikers are all alike, afraid to open your mouths. I guess we'd better send him to the Boys' Home, Joe, where they'll teach him his A-b-c. How about it, sonny?"

"What do you want to know?" spat out Romano.

"What you were doing in the room with Judge Somers when he was killed," Cusani shot back quickly.

"You can't hang that on me," whined Romano, now thoroughly frightened. "I wasn't near there."

"Oh yes, you were. We have a witness who saw you. You left your gun there and your finger-prints. This is no frame-up. It's the goods and the chair. What do you say Romano? Coming across clean?"

"It's a frame! It's a lousy frame!"

"No it isn't. I don't mind telling you why. We know all about it. You went up there to collect the money that the Judge promised you, for squealing on your own brother; you dirty two-timing rat!"

At this crowning insult, Romano launched himself at his tormentor, but, as he was hand-cuffed to the massive Blatchly, he did not get very far. He was forced back into his chair, white and helpless with fury.

Again Cusani took up the attack, inexorably, as he continued with a mocking smile, "Why, what's the matter? Everybody knows that's what you went up for. You don't have to be afraid. We can't send you up for that. It's true the papers may get hold of it and make a good story out of it. I can see the head-lines now 'Romano sold his brother for—' "

"Damn you shut up, I'll talk."

"We don't want to hear any fairy tales Romano. We know all about it. How much did he pay you?"

"You got to listen to me. You cops have got it all wrong. I'm goin' to tell you everything."

"All right if you want to," said Cusani, in the tone used to indulge a spoiled child. "But be quick about it because we want to go home to supper. Don't waste our time with any lies. We won't listen to you."

"This is straight," began Romano. "I seen him come out of the hotel and I follored him. I wanted to see him. He coulduv sprung me brudder and I was goin to ast him to. We was double-crossed in the city, Patsy an me. You knows I didn't do no squealing, Cusani." He waited for a reply.

"Go on," said Sallay as if greatly bored. "I can't wait all night. I am giving you your chance. Get going."

"Well, I ain't no squealer. When he got to the collitch one of them fly cops said someting to him and said where to meet him at six. So I goes to anudder gate where a friend of mine was and he let me in. I walked around wid de students and found out where he was. He was with a tall thin guy in a room. So I waited behind a door in the entry till he was alone. I waited a helluva while and the beak comes out and passes me an goes up de stairs. I was gointer follor, when de thin guy comes out and I ducks back. He goes out of the outside door, the one I was hiding behint. I was goin to go up again, when in comes dat fly cop and I ducks back again. De fly cop goes up but don't stay long. He comes down and beats it out fast. Den I gets my chance. I goes up and I finds a door open and there he was sitting by de window."

"Wait a minute," interrupted Cusani. "Was he wearing a hat?"

"Yeah, a black dip."

"All right. Go on."

"When he see me, he says, 'Whatjer want?' an I sez polite, 'Judge, you can spring me brudder. He is me twin an we was double-crossed. You sent him up for a long stretch.' He sez, 'Dis ain't no place to make no appeal. Come to my office in New York an I will hear it.' I was tired and my dogs hurted where I was standin all that time and I got kinder sore, so I sez, 'Yeah when I get to New York I'll get the same dirty deal you give Patsy.' So he says 'You're the man what wrote them letters. Get the hell outer here.' And I sez, 'You're not in New York now, you punk.' And then de big stiff hits me in de eye. So I pulls the rod to scare him. Honest to Gawd, Cusani, I wasn't going to drill him. But he makes anudder pass at me and grabs the gat. I tries to take it off of him and it goes off. He slides it in his pocket and laughs, then gives me a rush. I knocks the lid off him and beats it down the stairs and almost gets out of the building when another guy comes in and I ducks behind de same old door. Dis new guy sneaks up them stairs like a cat. He takes plenty of time. Goes up one step an waits, den anudder one an waits. You can't hear him. Pretty soon he gets to de top. I dassent move. That guy give me de heeby-jeebies. Der was somethin wrong about him. He was up there about five minutes and den comes pussy-footing down again. I had a good look at him through the crack in de door. So I gives him time to get away. I didn't want to see dat bird again. I was goin out again when two young fellows went up and yelled something and the thin guy comes in and runs up. Then he says some one was croaked and comes running down and goes to his room where de Judge was first. When I hears him telephoning to the cops, I beats it. And dat's Gawd's honest truth, Cusani."

Romano's story made a vivid impression on his audience. Cusani, whose eyes had never left the gangster's during the recital, was sure that they were listening to the truth. It also fitted in with the facts they had collected, too well to be a fabrication. Here, indeed, was the truth at last! He allowed none of his elation to show and asked perfunctorily, "Did you hear any shooting when this man was upstairs?"

"Hell, there was fireworks all the time. But I think there was one crack that sounded nearer then."

"Now then tell us who this last man was."

Romano's face set into a hard mask and he smiled coldly. "I ain't seen him before, copper."

"Well, what did he look like?"

"I don't know."

"Come on now, punk. You just said you had a good look at him. Tell me. What did he look like?"

"It was dark in there. I don't know."

"You lie! What did he look like?"

"I don't know."

"You do, damn you. You do know. What did he look like?"

"I don't know."

And despite anything that Cusani and Blatchly could do, short of resorting to physical force, they could get no other answer. They felt sure that Romano could identify the mysterious visitor but would not for some strong reason; either fear or a chance for possible blackmail.

Exhausted and weary they turned Romano back into his cell and checked out for the night.

"You're too easy, Sergeant," said Blatchly. "I can get that baby to talk. Leave him to me and you won't have to know anything about it."

"Sometimes I think that you are almost right, Joe. But I am not giving up. There's tomorrow and another tomorrow after that. I'll keep after him until he gives up. He can't last. I know those punks. He'll break down before long. Well I'm going; can I drop you anywhere?"

CHAPTER 12

THEY HAD RETURNED from the Judge's funeral and were seated in the library of the Somers' town house. One of the Judge's business partners, who was to read the will, had requested that Trout and Mather remain and they joined the relatives.

Mr. Haywood, the lawyer, rose and addressed them, "Judge Somers died a very wealthy man. His investments were all sound and even during the present depression, suffered little depreciation. This, his last will and testament, disposes of an estate of more than seven million dollars. It is holographic and I know that he spent considerable time over it."

He hemmed and, adjusting his spectacles carefully, began to read. After making provision for servants and office employees and various charities, the next item read, "To my distinguished friend Percival Trout, M.D., $100,000, in recognition of his early struggles and the benefits that he has given humanity since."

Those present looked at the astonished Trout with kindly smiles.

Mr. Haywood after a short pause continued, "To my very dear friend and companion in school and college, William Mather, $250,-000, as a slight remuneration for his kindnesses and great patience

in many matters during our association and his infallible guidance
in others known to him and me only. Also to the aforesaid William
Mather an additional sum of $100,000 to be held by him, the income
of which is to be disbursed for the benefit of one John Redfield personally known to him, the said William Mather."

Haywood paused again. There was a perceptible rustle, but no
evidence of curiosity or even astonishment on the faces of his well-
bred audience at this strange bequest.

There followed generous gifts to many relatives and to the University. The residue, which amounted to more than $5,000,000, was
left to the widow in trust for his two children and she and Dean
Mather were made joint executors.

Trout drove Mather back from New York. They said very little
for a long time; Trout busy at the wheel, guiding his powerful coupé
through the maze of early Sunday evening traffic and Mather absorbed in his own thoughts. It was not until they had passed through
the regular jam at Greenwich and were speeding down "Put's" Hill,
that Trout piped up, "That was damned decent of Somers to leave
me all that money, but I don't know what I am going to do with it.
I have more than I need now, from my salary and books."

"Why not get married, Percy?"

"Too busy, too old and not attractive enough. Besides that, the
few women that I have met are either too ugly if they have brains
and too dumb if they have good looks. I guess that I'll stick it out
the way I am now, although I saw a youngster yesterday who actually combined some sense with pulchritude. Want to hear about it?"

"Fire away, but I would rather hear what progress you have made
in finding Bert's murderer."

"Well, this is all part of it," said Trout and launched into a de-
tailed account of his experiences with Redfield and Elsie Fernaud.
His trained mind and retentive memory made it possible for him to
draw a very accurate picture. They were passing through Norwalk
before he had completed his recital. They continued on the Post
Road through Westport and it was not until they were climbing the
Green's Farm Hill, that Mather broke the silence.

"I want to tell you something, Percy. When we get to the top of
this hill, will you please pull over to the side of the road and park
there? I would like you to be able to give me your undivided attention."

Trout coasted silently to a stop on the hilltop and shut off the mo-
tor. He lighted a cigarette and inhaled deeply, waiting silently. He
felt Mather stirring uneasily beside him, evidently uncertain how to
begin and said kindly, "Look here, Bill, perhaps you would rather
not say anything. It will be perfectly all right with me and I will
understand."

"No, it isn't that. I was thinking—" He broke off abruptly and turned to face Trout. "You and I have been close friends for many years, Percy, and I think you will understand. Many nights while lying under the skies of far away lands, the desert of Arabia, the wastes of Thibet, the mountains of Honduras, I have watched those two stars take their course across the heavens. I always associated him with Pollux, the brighter and more prominent. In my mind he came always first. You may have thought it heartless or callous in me when on the night he was killed, I did not show more grief and chatted with you and Cusani, but I knew that he would not want me to do otherwise, just as he would want me to intrust to you the facts that I am about to tell you. It will explain much to you. As a matter of fact, Somers suggested himself, a month ago, that I should enlist your services in the problem which was giving him considerable worry. He had a high opinion of your abilities. I wish now that I had followed his suggestion, but I do not know whether it would have made any difference."

After a slight pause he continued, "I don't have to remind you of the close friendship that existed between Bert and myself. One day, it was in the fall in the beginning of our senior year, we had just left the old gym and were going to our rooms, when a girl stopped him and said she wanted to speak to him. To my surprise he asked me to excuse him and said he would meet me later in our quarters. He came in about an hour after. I was all ready to twit him about the affair, when I noticed that he was pale and haggard. He threw himself into a chair and said, 'Bill, I've got myself into a ghastly mess and I can't see how I can get out of it. If she would marry me, I would probably feel better. But she won't. She says that we would both be unhappy and that she would not stand in my way. She is scared to death, the poor kid. She says that her people are respectable and dote on her, an only child. It would break their hearts if they knew and unless she was able to go away soon, they could not help finding out. I don't even know her right name. She won't tell me.'

"The times have changed a lot since then. I suppose that our modern sophisticates, would have sneered at the two awe-struck boys whose world had been turned suddenly upside down. To us it was a tragedy, a cataclysm, how much so you can imagine when I tell you that *The Scarlet Letter* was thought by us to be inspired, and *Madam Bovary* something to be mentioned only in whispers. Two puritanical prigs? I don't think so. Put it down to our upbringing and the times before the Great War. Somers had only one thought, not for himself, he wasn't that kind, but for the girl. What could he do for her? He would have married her, knowing well that his people, while not approving of his choice, would never have shown her anything but kindness; they were too fine to behave in any other way. But she would not marry him. That to him would have been the only atonement, the only expiation. You, who knew him, must have recognized that trait in him. If he erred, he was the first to acknowledge the error and the readiest to make amends.

"He said that she wanted to go away at once, that she had a plan —had thought it all out. 'She knows a religieuse, a French sister, to whom she has confided her condition. This good woman has a brother who with his wife, is a care-taker of an estate in Brittany. Sister Elizabette is returning to France next month and has offered to take her back with her.'

"It seemed to me that it was a perfect solution of the problem, but Somers raised objections. He said it was unfair to the girl to ship her away surreptitiously. That she was taking all the punishment while he was getting off scot free. He was wealthy, and the expense meant nothing. It was no punishment for him. It took some time before he could be persuaded to accede. He went to New York and saw them off. On his return he told me that her secret had been discovered by her parents the night before. Due to the excitement of leaving and her condition, she had fainted and when the doctor was called, it was a secret no longer. She told Bert that they seemed stunned at first and then their only thought was for her welfare. There was no revilement, no censure, only love and affection. They would face the world together without shame. Their great fear was that she would leave them. She refused to let them make, what she considered, was a terrible sacrifice, for her. Next morning she had gone."

Mather paused, and taking out his pipe, filled it slowly. When he had lighted it, he went on, "The child was born that winter in France. The mother had a hard time of it, poor girl, but pulled through. Somers went over to see her that first summer and renewed his plea that she marry him if only for the child's sake. She was firm in her refusal, but agreed to have the child brought up under his supervision. He told me that she seemed indifferent to everything except hiding her identity. She said that her parents were in her mind constantly and she blamed herself for their desolation. She brooded over it. On his return, he wrote to her frequently. She never replied. The next year he went over again. He was then a student at the Harvard Law School. He found her in a pitiable mental state. Her mind had gone completely. He made what arrangements he could for her comfort and for the care of the child. When the child was five years old, Bert went over and brought him back with him. She raised no objections. He said that she looked younger than ever; liked to dress as a little girl and spent most of her time in the fields. Specialists declared that her case was incurable. Little could be done for her. She was getting every care and attention. The people were kindly and Somers paid them well. He did everything for her comfort. He paid the village doctor an annual retainer.

. The old parish priest was his correspondent."

Mather was silent for a full minute, then said simply "She died two months ago."

Trout leaned back and visualized the scene. A little Breton village, the simple peasants devoutly following the mortal remains of the sad stranger who had lived so long among them. The grave of the errant dove, far, far away from home and kin.

Mather went on, "Of course you know now who Redfield is. Yes, he was the child. Somers did everything that any one could for him but it was useless. He was a singular boy. He had no vices and no talents. Physically strong and handsome, morally a coward and colorless. You have seen him and know."

Trout nodded. "Yes, I know; hopeless."

"That was Bert's cross. Redfield had no sense of responsibility. No ambitions, no recourse. He was simply a mere nonentity, the direct antithesis of Somers himself. After flunking one school after another, Somers found him various jobs which he was unable to hold for more than a month at a time. He then asked me to help and I got him his present work at the University where I could keep an eye on him. He has held it now for three years and is perfectly happy in it. Ostensibly Somers was his guardian. Whether or not he suspects a closer relationship, I don't know. I believe he does but is perfectly indifferent about it. As long as he gets the generous allowance Somers allots him, he is satisfied."

They sat silently watching the long lines of coruscant head lights hurtling toward them in ceaseless procession. A whizz and a phut, as the passenger cars rushed by; a growl and a roar from the massive trucks. Here came an inter-urban bus, like a terrestrial ferry boat, port and starboard lights burning and the interior brilliantly illuminated, crowded with tired passengers.

There went a sleek dark luxury, purring its smooth efficiency past her humbler sisters. They caught a momentary glimpse of two uniformed servants and a solitary fur-swathed old man. Then came a car with a single head-light, coughing and clattering and almost overflowing with singing happy-go-lucky youngsters. Then another and another, some whizzing by silently, others with laughter and shrieks. The Sunday hordes returning to the man-made cliffs of the great city. A cross-section of our American Democracy.

"Well," said Mather, knocking the ashes out of his pipe, "I think that is all."

"Do you want to tell me why Somers suggested that you should tell me the story?" asked Trout.

"Yes, I omitted that. She never told him her name and he thought that if her people were in need, he might be able to do something for them. He felt sure that you could find out."

"I think that she was wiser than he was. Better leave that alone," said Trout as he snapped on the ignition.

CHAPTER 13

"I THINK THAT I SHOULD SEE REDFIELD and explain my position under Somers' will to him," said Dean Mather to Professor Trout Monday morning. "And unless you are busy, perhaps it would be well for you to come with me."

"I haven't a thing to do until the fall. I gave my final lecture for the term last week and Cartwright can carry on with the tests. I'll telephone to the garage for the car and while we are waiting, you might clear up a point for me. When you went into the room, just after Somers was killed, did you touch or move anything?"

Mather hesitated, then answered slowly, "I don't remember. I may have. Things were rather confused for the moment and I had received a bad shock. However, I do remember that I cautioned Bob and Gregory not to touch anything; therefore, it is not likely that I did. Why? Is it important?"

"Well, yes, it might be; but I don't want to influence you with any suggestions from me, if you can't remember yourself. So let's forget it. Cusani telephoned a little while ago to say that he was coming to see me after luncheon. He sounded as if he was bursting with news. He intimated that Romano had talked and given him something to sink his teeth into. He also said that he had seen young Gregory, but refused to go into details until his visit later today. He was quite mysterious about it."

The captain in charge of the campus police had told them that Redfield was off duty and they were driving to his home, when a minatory wail, rapidly increasing in volume, caused Trout to pull over toward the curb as a small black coupé shrieked past.

"That was Cusani," he said, steering back into the road, "and in a hell of a hurry."

They had not gone far, when with more howling two additional cars roared by.

"Donovan and the head-quarters staff," said Trout, with a startled look at Mather. "Good God, it can't be that—" He did not finish but speeded up in the wake of the others, the official sirens clearing the way before them.

Trout's fears were confirmed as the Chief turned into the street where Redfield lived. Parked in front of the house was Cusani's coupé. They piled out quickly and rushed through the open door into the house, Trout leading the way to Redfield's rooms. They halted, spellbound, at the door, by the strange tableau which met their startled gaze.

Lying on the floor dead, was the body of John Redfield; an unpleasant mass which even the dignity of death failed to enshroud with reverence. Even now in the greatest moment of his futile career, the center of the stage was stolen from him.

All eyes were fixed on two vibrant figures struggling in close contact; Elsie Fernaud and Sergeant Cusani. She was beating his chest with tightly closed fists, her round firm breasts heaving under her knitted jacket, her black eyes blazing furiously.

"You did!" she cried. "You did! You lied. You said he was safe. You promised him. You did. You did!"

She collapsed suddenly and sank into his arms with gasping sobs. "I trusted you. Oh how could you? How could you?"

Cusani led her gently to the divan and then stepped to the center of the room and surveyed the astonished group at the door coldly as he muttered, "If I hear a crack from any of you wise guys, there'll be another killing."

"But Sally, what the—" spluttered the mystified Donovan.

"She says we did it," cut in Cusani.

"We? Who do you mean? We?"

"Why we," reiterated the Sergeant irritably. "We, the police."

"The police?" gasped Donovan. "Why Sally, she's—"

"I know. It's screwy. She's got it all wrong. But that's what she said."

He looked at them truculently, his hands in his coat pockets. "Oh come on in. It's only another murder."

He fixed his eyes on Trout and Mather and frowned.

"Come on in, Major," he said bitterly. "Bring your friend with you. You might find a few more hats."

When they had entered, he addressed Donovan.

"I picked up the police broadcast and got here a minute or so before you. I found Redfield lying there dead. Miss Fernaud, this young lady here, accused the police of killing him. That's all I know and brings you all up to date. How did you and Dean Mather get here so soon, Major Trout?"

Trout started to explain, but Cusani cut him short.

"It makes no difference. Perhaps it's for the best after all."

He scanned the group and asked, "Where's Blatchly, Chief?"

"I left him down at headquarters. He had just come in. I thought you wanted to keep him on the Somers case, Sally."

"The Somers case!" ejaculated the impatient Sergeant. "Why, what do you think—Never mind. I see that you have brought Sam Lucas with you instead. Now is there anything that you would like to suggest, Chief?"

"No Sally, not a thing, not a thing. How did the poor fellow get killed?"

"I don't know yet. There's no blood or anything. She said some one conked him on the dome. I'm waiting for Doc Mansfield to make an examination when he gets here. In the meantime, Major, will you be so good as to assist Miss Fernaud from the room? This is no place for her."

Elsie rose and walked out saying that she needed no assistance but would go to her room and lie down. She would be there, at their call when needed to tell her story.

Mansfield came in at that moment. After a careful examination he rose and dusting off his hands, looked at Donovan superciliously as he said, "I suppose you want to know the 'hows' and 'whens'? Well, here they are, if it will do you any good. He was killed by a blow on the back of his head by some heavy object possibly that iron smoking-stand, lying over there. It was a powerful blow. The base of the skull is crushed in. I'm giving it to you in plain language. If you want the technical trimmings, I am certain that my brilliant colleague, Dr. Trout, will be glad to translate. It is impossible for the blow to have been self-inflicted. I can't tell when it happened, for it is possible for him to have lived hours after it; and on the other hand, it might have killed him instantaneously. He died less than an hour ago. I'll send the morgue wagon for him and notify the coroner. Well, gentlemen, it's getting to be quite a habit. What? Have you any more hidden away? If so, please trot them out now because I'm busy. What? No more? Well, cheerio, then."

Donovan groaned and turned to Cusani. "We got to do something Sally. The mayor was sore this morning because I couldn't satisfy him on the Somers case and here is this one right on top of it. He's going to be awful sore now and perhaps call in outside help. What do you think Doc Mansfield meant about a habit?"

"Ask Professor Trout over there. He told me once that some smart bird said 'Murder is a habit.' We may expect several more before we are through."

Donovan moaned miserably, "Oh my God, Oh my God, and now they will suspect the department. I don't dare to look at the papers any more. It's awful. This is the worst thing that has happened during my administration. Two murders in less than a week. You got to do something Sally. You certainly got to do something."

"We are doing all that can be done," said Cusani with no effort to control his contempt. "Is there anything that you would like to suggest, Chief?"

"No, Sally. I leave it all to you. But we got to get some results. I'm going now. You don't need me here any more. I'll leave Sam Lucas with you. That Doc Mansfield—and I always thought he was my friend too. He can be awful mean, can't he? Well—So long, folks."

Donovan's departure was the signal for activity. Cusani had the photographer and fingerprint man busy, while he and Lucas were looking about. Trout examined the ashes on the floor and rug. He picked up some paper matches and put them in an envelope which he returned to his pocket. The iron smoking stand was subjected to a minute scrutiny and yielded a few hairs which matched those of the dead man. It was free from fingerprints.

"That's the weapon all right," said Cusani. "It's been wiped clean which makes it a certainty. What do you think, Major?"

"You are probably right."

"And that's about all there is. Not another thing to show except this cigar butt. Any prints around, Elmer?"

"Only Redfield's, Sergeant, and a few that might be the girl's."

"All right. When you get through here, you and Melvin can go. Sam, will you take care of the smoking stand? When the hearse comes, let them take the body. Leave one of the cops in here and you go and see if you can get anything out of any one in the house. Try the servants. I'm going to get Miss Fernaud's story. Will you come with me, Major?" He paused and then added, "Dean Mather can come along too, if he wants to."

"No," said the Dean, "I would only be in the way. I'll go out and wait for you in the car."

Elsie came down to the living room where Cusani and Trout were waiting for her. She appeared calm. She smiled wanly at the Sergeant as she held out her hand and said, "I am sorry, Mr. Cusani. It seems that I must always be apologizing to you."

"Please don't let it disturb you. Our work is often very unpleasant and it makes it doubly so, when we are compelled to upset nice people. I am afraid that even now we are taking a great liberty, but I know that you want to help us in every possible way to clear up this killing of your friend. I feel guilty myself about it. After our visit here Saturday, I withdrew the man I had watching him. There didn't seem to be any further need for him. Well, it's too late now for anything except recriminations and they never help any one. Will you please tell us, Miss Fernaud, what you know about this?"

The girl looked at Cusani soberly as she said, "This is not going to be pleasant for you, but please believe me that I now do not think that you are involved personally."

She paused as if uncertain how to proceed, then drawing herself up and with her face set in hard stern lines, her eyes flashing, she announced, *"I accuse the police of the murder of John Redfield!"*

There was a dead silence. The two men stirred uncomfortably under her dramatic indictment.

Cusani finally shook his head. "No, that is impossible," he said.

"It is true, nevertheless."

"But how could—" began Sally.

Trout signaled him to stop and turned to the girl. "Of course, Miss Fernaud," he said, "you are speaking figuratively."

"I am not. He was actually murdered by the police."

"But how could you possibly know?"

"He told me so himself, just before he died."

"He told you himself?" gasped the bewildered Sergeant.

"Perhaps Miss Fernaud had better tell us all about it," suggested Trout. "May I ask you Miss Fernaud, to think carefully of everything, no matter how unimportant it may seem to you, that took place today and tell us. For instance, you might start with what you did after breakfast."

"I went downtown to do my marketing."

"Had you seen Redfield before that?"

"Yes, at the breakfast table. He used to drive me down in his car whenever he had a day off; but this morning, he told me to use the car myself as he was expecting a caller. I returned at about a quarter to ten. As I passed his door, I heard voices and smelled tobacco smoke, so I went right on and was busy with my regular morning household duties. It must have been somewhere between half past ten and a quarter to eleven when I passed the door again. I thought that I heard a moan and stopped. It was repeated and came from Johnny's room. I called to him—asked him if he was sick. When I received no reply, I opened the door and—and I saw him lying there on the floor. He seemed to be quite conscious. He was muttering as if he was trying to convey some message to me. I kneeled down at his side and asked, 'What is it, Johnny? What's the trouble?' He mumbled incoherently, but I caught some words clearly. 'Somers' and 'mother,' or maybe 'Mather,' and then, 'It's finished. The cops finished me.' "

She stopped for a moment as Trout and Cusani looked at each other aghast.

"It was not until then," she continued, "that I realized how serious his condition really was. There was nothing to indicate what had happened. No wound or blood. The only thing out of the way was the smoking stand lying near him, which I thought he had knocked over when he fell. I rushed out for help. Doctor Garret was running down the stairs. He had been calling on mother. He was in a great hurry and when I stopped him, said that he had just received an emergency call from the hospital and could not be delayed. However, I half dragged him into the room. When he saw Johnny, he became very serious and made a quick examination. When he finished, he looked at me strangely and said, 'This man is dead, Elsie. The back of his head has been caved in. There is nothing that I can do here. I'd like to stay and help you, but my first duty is to the living. I'll telephone the police for you and tell them where they can reach me, if they want me.' That is all I know."

"Do you feel that you are strong enough to answer a few very necessary questions?" inquired Trout gently.

"Yes, I want to help."

"Did Redfield tell you with whom he had made the appointment?"

"No. I thought it rather strange too as he usually confided in me."

"And here is another strange thing, Miss Elsie. We three know how obsessed he was by a fear that the police would torture him. One might assert now that those fears were justified, but to me that would clear the police of any complicity in this terrible affair."

"How do you make that out?" asked Cusani hopefully.

"From the fact that he made the appointment at all. We must use common sense. When we called here Saturday, he would not see us except in the presence of a witness. Miss Fernaud told us that he stood in deathly fear of the police. Do you think that in the face of that, he would make what amounted to a secret appointment with them? No. You know he would not. He would have told Miss Elsie all about it. This meeting was with some one whom he knew well."

"But, Dr. Trout," protested Elsie, "he said that it was the police."

"That may be explained in several ways. He was semi-conscious, his obsession may have been uppermost in his waning mind, he may have tried to say something else and the words became paragogic and Miss Fernaud may have misunderstood their meaning. There may be other reasons of which we know nothing."

"No," said the girl decidedly, "I am quite sure. He said, 'The *cops* finished me.' "

There was a knock on the door. Detective Lucas entered and reported to Cusani. "I've talked to everybody in the house except a sick lady upstairs and haven't found nothing. There was a big blonde who may have seen something, but I don't believe her. I think she's a goof, because when I asked her who she was, she said she was the Admiral and had charge of all the vessels on the—Ouch! Stop kicking me, Sergeant," he yelled as he rubbed his bruised shin.

"I have heard that before," said Elsie unperturbed. "That was Thelma. She is our new chambermaid. She isn't very bright, but has a great opinion of her own sense of humor."

"May we talk to her?" asked Cusani.

"Yes, of course. If there is nothing more you want of me, I will go up to my mother. She must be worried. I will send Thelma in to you."

Thelma Andersen was a well rounded blonde Juno. A perfect Nordic type physically. Strikingly handsome with her heavy mass of honey-colored hair coiled around her head, her pink cheeks and blue eyes. But, when she opened her mouth, all that majestic beauty slid into it. She was transformed into a butcher shop. Her blood-red gums almost covered her small irregular teeth, her lips looked like a cut of thick steak. Even her body seemed to change into something one sees hanging in a refrigerator. Trout classified her as a "wholk" which was a degree higher than a "glomph."

She came in grinning at Lucas, who indicated Cusani with a wave of his hand and said, "Tell the Sergeant what you told me."

"I told him to behave like a gentleman and stop pawing me," was the astonishing answer.

The red-faced Lucas started for her with a furious retort, but she backed away tauntingly and said, "He tried to make me, but I ain't got no use for no Polskies."

"Sit down, Sam," barked Sally, "and leave that girl alone. Sit down, Miss. No one is going to try any funny business while I am here."

She sat down seemingly a little disappointed. She smiled at the three men and said, "What do you fellows want? I got a lot of work to do so you'd better make it snappy."

"We want to ask you some questions," said Cusani. "I suppose you know that one of the lodgers here has been killed? We are investigating his death and we hope that you may be able to help us."

"Yeah, I know, that Redfield. He tried to get next the first time he saw me. I was making his bed—"

"We are not interested in what he tried to do, Thelma," broke in Cusani hurriedly. "We have lots of work to do ourselves. As you said, let's make it snappy. Some other time, perhaps, you can tell me about it."

She looked at the Sergeant appraisingly. "Well," she said, "I might fall for you at that. What do you want to know?"

"Did you admit any one to the house this morning?"

"No. I was upstairs when the bell rang and, before I could get down, that Redfield must have answered. I heard him say, 'Come in.' They went to his room."

"What time was that?"

"About half past nine."

"Did you see who it was that came in?"

"No, but I seen him when he went out."

"You did? When was that?"

"I heard Miss Elsie come in from her marketing and looked at the clock. It was quarter of ten. About half an hour after that, I heard the front door slam shut. I was doing up the big front room over this, so I went to the window to see who had went out."

"That's fine, Thelma," said the Sergeant elated. "Go on, tell us who he was."

"I don't know. He was a tall skinny guy and he was getting in his car."

"What kind of a car?"

"One of them new flivs that the cops use, like that one standing in front of the house now." She pointed at Cusani's car parked at the curb.

"That's fine, but doesn't help much. There are a lot of cars like that in town."

"Yeah, but this one had letters printed on it too," she said with a grin.

Cusani frowned and asked, "Could you read them?"

"No. He beat it too quick."

"Perhaps," he suggested hopefully, "you read the license plate numbers?"

"If you'd only told me ahead of time, I might of. But you didn't, so I didn't."

"That's too bad, Thelma," said Sally patiently. "Can you give us any further description of him? How was he dressed?"

"He had on a uniform. I thought he was a copper first, but I ain't so sure. Maybe he was and maybe he wasn't. He had a cap on and a badge. He had something shining in his hand."

Cusani looked worried. "How old would you say he was?"

"Gee, I don't know, mister. He wasn't too old and he wasn't too young; about half way. How òld are you?"

Sally ignored the question and glanced at Trout who took up the examination.

"You say that he slammed the door?"

"Yes, he slammed it hard. You could hear it all over the house."

"And that was at about twenty minutes past ten?"

"Yes, mister, maybe later, perhaps half past."

Trout turned to Cusani and said, "Will you please find Miss Fernaud and ask her if she heard the door slam? If possible, you might check the time."

When the Sergeant hurried out, Thelma looked at Trout and asked, "What's the matter with you fellows. Don't you believe me?"

"Oh yes, we believe you," said Trout. "But it is always best to seek corroboration."

"I believe in that too," she said. "Do you live here in town?"

"Yes. I have lived here all my life," he answered, amused.

"Well, I don't know many fellows here. I come from Branford. I like the movies, don't you?"

"No, I can't say that I do," said Trout, smiling. "Now Mr. Lucas, over there, is extremely fond of them and I am sure never misses a good picture when it comes to town. I have often seen him going to them alone. Yes, all alone."

"Say," shouted the bewildered Lucas, "what are you handing out? I never go to no movies. I think they're lousy."

"Ah," said Thelma, "he's only a Polski. He would be like that."

Cusani returned with Elsie, much to Trout's relief.

"Miss Fernaud wanted to tell you herself about the door slamming," said Sally.

"Yes, Dr. Trout, I did hear the front door slam. It was that that brought me into the hall."

"According to your and Thelma's opinions, that must have been about half past ten o'clock. Is that right?"

"Yes, as near as I can place it. Do you think that that was the murderer?"

"No, I don't. I am almost sure that it wasn't, but I would like to know who it was. He might be able to help us."

He described the man whom Thelma had seen leaving the house and inquired if Elsie could place him. After some further questioning she shook her head and said that no one of that description was known to her.

"One more question, please, Miss Fernaud," said Trout. "Did Redfield ever smoke cigars?"

"No, I am sure he didn't, Dr. Trout."

"Thank you, ladies. That is all for the present, unless Sergeant Cusani has something else to ask."

When they were alone again, Cusani said, "Let's go to your rooms and get this straightened out. There's something that I can't make out. If that guy who drove off after slamming the door, wasn't the killer, who in hell was he?"

"I don't know," said Trout. "But come on, let's get going. Mather must be tired waiting. He has something to tell you that may surprise you and you haven't told me yet about your talk with Romano and Gregory. We can go to my rooms and I'll have sandwiches and beer brought in so we won't waste time in going out for luncheon."

"That suits me fine. I'll follow you in a few minutes. I want to call up headquarters and take care of some details here first."

"Oh, and Sally, don't forget to bring that cigar stub with you, when you come."

CHAPTER 14

THEY MADE A HASTY LUNCHEON. Cusani, uneasy and fidgety, picked at the food. He moved about, nervous, restless. Two mysterious murders with few clues to their perpetrator. There was a ruthless, implacable killer loose in the community. One who, without fear and in broad daylight, with an apparent disregard of apprehension or concealment, had struck twice. A hideous cobra who slipped in and out leaving no trace of his identity.

Would he strike again? If so, where? And at whom? Who was safe from the next attack? Were these two tragedies the deeds of a madman or were they part of a well-defined plan, actuated by some inexorable will behind which lay some unknown motive? What connection was there, if any, between Judge Somers' murder and that of the fatuous Redfield? What possible reason could exist that made it necessary that these two men, so far removed from each other in their stations in life, should meet their death at the hands of a common executioner?

Why had Redfield gone to see the Judge? Had he seen the killer there? Had the killer seen him? Who was the mysterious, tall, thin man that Thelma had seen leaving the house? Why had Trout absolved him so readily? What was Dean Mather doing so soon on the scene of the two crimes?

He remembered now that there was something important that he must ask Mather. Trout, too, had said that Mather had some surprising disclosure to make. Cusani felt that Trout was holding back important information which would be of help and he resented it. He intended to call for a show-down. This was no time for concealment and a mistaken sense of loyalty. A savage murderer was abroad. It was the duty of every one, no matter what might come of it, to give every possible help to the police. Whenever Mather's name had come up, Trout had become taciturn and had shelved him off on something else. That was going to be changed right now. He would permit no further evasions. If he could not get all the cards on the table now, he would take steps that might endanger a long and devoted friendship.

He glanced thoughtfully at his old friend, then turned abruptly to Mather.

"The Major said that you had something that you wanted to tell me."

"Yes, Sergeant," retorted the Dean. "It was about Redfield. I think you should be told that he was Judge Somers' son."

"Oh, he was, was he?" exclaimed Cusani bitterly. "And what does that make me? 'The mottled-faced man'?"

"Why, what do you mean?" asked the astonished Mather.

"I mean just this. There has been too damn much pussy-footing going on in this case. You and Trout have been withholding information that is vital to me and some of your actions are open to criticism, if not suspicion. No, Major, this time please do not interrupt. This is going to be the show-down. I have gone this far and I'm not going to let you or any one else stand in my way. You and the Dean have not been shooting square and you will either come clean now, or I will take other measures to make you."

"I am sorry, Sally," said Trout, "that you are taking this attitude. I warned you repeatedly to steer clear of this angle. You are making a bad mistake. However, if that is your decision, I won't try to do anything to change it. I feel sure that Dean Mather is of the same opinion."

"Hold on there, Trout," said Mather steadily. "Speak for yourself. I don't need any one to fight my battles, nor have I anything to conceal. I cannot blame Cusani for complaining that I have not been entirely open with him so far. I haven't. I may plead in justification that the secret of Redfield's birth was not mine to divulge. Now, that both Somers and Redfield are dead, I see no harm in telling it to him in confidence. How it will help him, or what it has to do with their murders, I cannot conceive."

"It may have everything to do with them," said the Sergeant, "or nothing at all. Just the same, I thank you, even at this late date. Now, that you have expressed a desire to be of help, perhaps you will answer a few questions."

"Exactly what do you want to know, Sergeant?"

"You might tell me first, what it was that you picked up from the floor of the room in which Judge Somers was killed."

Mather frowned in a puzzled manner and answered, "It is odd that you should ask me that."

"Why?"

"Because Trout asked me the same question this morning."

"He did, eh?" Cusani raised his eyebrows. "Well, what's the answer?"

"The answer is the same as I told Trout. I do not remember that I picked up anything."

"Are you sure?"

"No, I am not. I was under a severe strain at the moment and somewhat confused."

"It would not surprise you then, if I had a witness who will swear to the fact that he saw you picking something from the floor?"

"No, it would not surprise me. Who was it?"

"I don't mind telling you. I talked with young Gregory and he told me. He said that after you had examined the body, you rose and stepped backwards, then stooped down and—"

"By jove, you are right, Cusani," exclaimed the Dean. "I stepped back and tripped over something, picked it up and placed it on the table."

"What was it?"

"A black derby hat."

"Aha!" shouted Trout. "That's it. That's how it happened. Look here, Mather, show us where that hat was lying. Here—wait a minute—mark the place on this rough plan I have drawn of the room. Right there, eh? That's perfect. Well, that establishes the time factor and all we need to do now is—"

"The time factor!" shouted Cusani. "Cripes, Percy, I forgot all about that. Why, I've got a witness who saw the whole parade. He was hiding behind the section entry door and saw everything."

"What do you mean 'everything'? The murder?"

"No, of course not. But I'm sure he saw the murderer."

"Who was it?" demanded Trout.

"I don't know yet. Perhaps I'd better tell you about it. That mutt, Romano, was waiting behind the door to head off the Judge. He said he wanted to see him regarding his twin brother. He can't get at him because he is busy with the Dean. He sees the Judge go up-stairs and Mather go out. Then he sees Redfield go up and run out again. He goes up himself. He said he had a fight with the Judge during which he pulled a gun. Somers took it away from him, but it was exploded during the scuffle. The Judge puts it in his pocket and kicks him out. As he is beating it, he hears some one else com-ing and ducks behind the door again. He sees this last guy sneaking upstairs where he stays about five minutes and then come sneaking down once more. Before he can get away, the two young fellows come in and then Dean Mather. He hears Gregory call the Dean and from the talk surmises that some one has been killed. After the Dean comes down to telephone, he hot-foots it as fast as he can. That was when Finn, at the portal, saw him running out. There's the complete time-table for you, and I think it is correct."

He looked at his two amazed listeners and smiled at Trout.

"How does that check with you, Major?"

"Practically perfect, Sally. I had already placed Redfield and Romano in that order; that is *before* the murder was committed. The third man I was not so sure about. Of course he was the mur-derer."

Cusani sat silently for a while and then turning to the Dean, said, "Do you agree with that, Dean Mather?"

"Why yes. It seems obvious, doesn't it?"

"Yes, it does, but it is not proven. It isn't like the Major to jump to conclusions so quickly either. What makes you so sure that this unknown man did it, Major?"

"Perhaps I was a little too precipitate that time, Sally. Thanks for reminding me. It fits with the theory that I had evolved and that was the reason for my statement. You undoubtedly may prove me wrong. What's the matter with it?"

"I won't say that you are wrong, Major. But you are the one that taught me never to accept anything as a fact until every other pos-sibility has been exhausted. The man may have found Somers dead already when he entered the room, or he could have been mur-dered by some one else while he was up there. No, Major, I am by no means ready to scrap every other possibility yet."

"All right, Sally. I think I know what is biting you and we might as well have it out now. Come on and get it out of your system."

"Here it is then. I have never been satisfied with the disappearance of the fatal bullet. Now, the murderer may have picked it up to prevent our matching it with his revolver, if it ever came into our possession, or he may have had another reason."

"What other reason could there be, Sergeant?" inquired Mather.

"It may not have been a revolver bullet at all. It may have been something more easily traced, more damnably incriminating. A rifle bullet."

"A rifle bullet? But would not a man with a rifle be rather conspicuous on the campus?"

"No one says that he appeared on the campus with it. The rifle may have been aimed by a good marksman from a position across the quadrangle and hit the Judge as he was standing by the open window. Are you sure, Dean Mather, that when you picked up the hat by Judge Somers' body, you did not pick up a rifle bullet also?"

As the full import of Cusani's questions were made manifest to his comprehension, Mather showed a flash of anger which quickly gave way to a look of incredulous dismay. He glanced uncertainly at Trout, who made an effort to smile staunchly. Then he turned back to Cusani.

"If I understand you correctly, Sergeant," he said calmly, "you are accusing me of having killed Judge Somers."

"No, Dean, I am not. I am not accusing anybody. But, you must admit that there are circumstances which must be explained before we can get much further on. I know that you and Major Trout are thinking that I am merely a dumb cluck and it may turn out that I am. You probably won't believe me when I tell you that this has been worrying me for several days. Trout must have suspected it, but the fact that he did not tip you off to what was coming, proves to me that he did not put much belief in it. If he thought that you were guilty, he would have given you the word in New York and you would have been on your way to Guatemala or Honduras by this time. No, Dean Mather, in spite of all the fingers pointing at you, I find it hard to believe that you killed those two men."

"Thank you, Cusani," said Mather quietly. "I wonder if you have time to tell me precisely what these incriminating circumstances are?"

"That's exactly what I want to do, so that you can explain them and we can clean up this angle which has interfered with the orderly progress the Major and I were making. The possibility that the first murder could have been committed with a rifle, destroys what alibi you may have had by being absent from the immediate scene. You are a good marksman, are you not?"

"Yes, I can claim that I am."

"Do you own a rifle?"

"Yes, several."

"Where are they?"

"They are packed away in their cases except one which I had out Thursday morning at the rifle-range and which I took back to my room to clean."

"Will you please get it?"

"Sorry, Sergeant. I can't, I don't know where it is."

"You don't know where it is?" repeated Cusani aghast. "What do you mean by that?"

Trout started to interrupt but thought better of it when Cusani frowned at him and turned to Mather for his explanation.

"I will admit that it makes the situation look much blacker for me," said Mather with a wry smile, "but that is the case. The rifle is missing. I got up early this morning to go to the range for a little practice and I could not find it."

"What did you do then?" asked Cusani.

"I went out there anyway, thinking that some one may have borrowed it while I was in New York, but there was no one out there. So I drove around the country a bit and came back here."

"What car did you drive?"

"I called up the garage and they told me that one of the new cars which had been ordered for the expedition, had been delivered and wanted to know if I would like to try it out, so I told them to send it around."

"What kind of a job was it?"

"A black coupé. A small one."

"Was it marked? Did it have any lettering on it?"

"Why, yes it was. It was marked, 'Mather Mayan Expedition,' on the door."

"Did you make any stops when you were driving around? Did you see anybody you knew?"

"No, I do not think that I did."

"What time did you get back here?"

"I don't know exactly. I drove the car back to the garage and told them to make certain necessary adjustments, and then walked over here to Trout's room."

"What for?"

"I wanted him to come over to Redfield's with me. I wanted to tell Redfield about Judge Somers' will."

"Yes, go on please."

"We drove over in Trout's car. You passed us on the avenue and we arrived at the same time as the police. I think that is all."

"And it's plenty," said Cusani mordaciously. "I wonder if you realize how deeply you have involved yourself. Let me tell you. There was your silence about Redfield, then your rooms are directly opposite the one in which the Judge was killed, you are a crack shot, there's the missing rifle, the missing bullet·which you could have picked up. Your action with the hat was open to suspicion to say nothing of your lapse of memory regarding it. Then there is your morning drive, with no witnesses in a car which was described as leaving Redfield's house just after the murder and finally, there is the description of a man which fits you perfectly, who drove off in that identical car. Don't you see that instead of explaining anything, you have only made matters much worse for yourself?"

"So it appears," said Mather calmly. "But why should I kill my best friend? There must have been a motive."

"Certainly, there must have been a motive," acknowledged the Sergeant. "I don't know of one at the present moment, I'll admit; but one will be shown. It always is."

Cusani sat silent thinking for a short time, his elbow on the table, his chin in his cupped hand. Finally he raised his eyes and addressed Mather again.

"You mentioned a will a little while ago. The Judge's will, you said. Who were the beneficiaries?"

"I was one," answered Mather without hesitation. "He left me $250,000."

"$250,000? A quarter of a million?" shouted the startled Cusani, and added bitingly, "Is that all?"

"No," replied the Dean steadily. "He also left $100,000 to me as a trust for Redfield."

"$100,000 more in trust for Redfield," gasped the Sergeant as he leaned back in his chair. "And we wanted a motive. Good God!"

There was a dead silence, each man deeply immersed in his own thoughts, a portentous hush as if foreboding some dire calamity. It was shattered by the strident ringing of the telephone bell.

Trout rose to answer it. After a moment's talk, he turned and said wearily, "It's for you Sally. Chief Donovan wants to talk to you."

Cusani picked up the receiver and said, "Yes, Chief, this is Sally ... What? ... Christ ... Hold everything, Chief. I'll be right over."

He braced himself with both his hands clenched on the table, the knuckles showing white against the sunbrown backs and announced in a hoarse whisper, "They have just found Romano dead in his cell. His head is bashed in."

CHAPTER 15

THE DINGY old headquarters building was seething with excitement when Trout and Cusani rushed up the steps. Chief Donovan, for once stirred into activity, was barking orders right and left and reversing himself east and west. Policemen, detectives, clerks, reporters and ordinary civilians were milling about in confusion. A look of relief passed over the face of the harried Chief as he saw Cusani entering.

"He's in back, in the cell," he called. He was white around the mouth and beads of sweat glistened on his forehead; his eyes were bulging.

When the Sergeant approached closer, he whispered hoarsely, "I went back there with Doc Mansfield. God, I wish I had stayed away . . . I ain't feeling none too good . . . I got sick and had to go to the toilet . . . When I came back, some one let all these people in. My God, Sally, there's going to be an awful stink about this thing." He turned to the crowded room and shouted, "Here, you folks, you all gotta get out of here."

"Wait a minute, Chief," said Cusani, "let me take care of this . . . You, Smith and Turner, get this room cleared at once or I'll have your shields. Those who belong in the building, go to your proper places. You newspaper people can wait in the hall until we have something for you. Everybody else . . . out in the street and make it snappy."

Order was quickly restored under Cusani's supervision and he returned to the panting Donovan.

"Okay now, Chief, I'm ready. Do you want to tell us about it now or later?"

"No, not now, Sally. You'd better wait here for Doc Mansfield. He ought to be through pretty soon. P'raps he can tell us something . . . I ain't going back there again . . . I seen all I want to . ."

Mansfield came in from the cell corridor. He was drying his hands on a towel and shaking his head. When he saw Trout and Cusani he grinned with a ghoulish leer.

"Oh there you are! I was wondering why you two great criminologists weren't doing some master-minding on the scene before. I left your friend Blatchly back there. He was popping his biscuit." He looked at Donovan and sniffed. "Phew! Well, this one is dead too; dead as the Ten Commandments. Look him over when you find time, but I warn you that he isn't a pretty sight. Don't take my word for

77

it. Ask the Chief, Ha! Ha! His head is beaten to a jelly—a mush. His brains are leaking out like— Don't go, Chief, I want to tell you that you can send it down to the morgue when you get through with it. Well, that makes two for the day so far. I should think that you cops would begin to get peeved, or don't you care? Aren't you afraid that this killer might come in and lift his leg at you? Oh yes, he's been dead about an hour. I must admit that you find them quick enough, but this one was right under your noses. Can you see the headlines, 'Police Protected Prisoner Punched to Pulp'? What do you say, Trout? *Quis custodiet ipsos custodes?*"

"Don't air your cheap witticisms on me, Mansfield," retorted Trout, and added, *"ne sutor supra crepidan."*

"Ho! Ho!" roared Mansfield. "Take that to yourself, my Trout," and left the room chuckling.

"God, Sally," groaned Donovan. "What are we going to do? What will every one say? They will blame this one on us sure. We're in wrong on the Redfield killing already and then this one . . . Right under our noses, as the Doc says."

"Don't let it worry you, Chief," said Cusani. "Why don't you go to your office and lock the door and take a little rest, while the Major and I go and look the ground over? When we come back you can tell us all about it."

Donovan sighed and looked gratefully at the Sergeant. "I think I will, if you are sure you don't need me. Doc Mansfield upset me something awful."

They found the photographer and the finger-print man leaving the cell. Both looked pale and shaken.

"Not a trace, not even his own prints. You'll see why when you go in," reported Elmer.

"Okay, thanks," said Cusani, and they entered the cell.

In the center of the little old-fashioned room stood Blatchly livid and quaking. The white-washed walls were dyed crimson; the floor was sticky, viscous, glutinous, horrible. Huddled in a farther corner was the body of the dead Romano; a pitiful, small heap, cheap and repulsive, its face a shocking abomination. Accustomed as they were to sudden death in many forms, the brutality evinced in this one was execrable to them. Even Cusani, with all the loathing he had had for what the gangster represented, felt a surge of compassion come over him.

"My God, Sally," whispered Trout hoarsely. "What beast did this?"

"Hush," breathed Cusani softly. "Did you hear that?"

"What?" murmured Trout, looking up. He saw Blatchly crossing himself hurriedly and then— He heard it too! A thin whimpering wail like the cry of a frightened child— "Help . . . Help! Let me out . . . Dear Jesus . . . Let me out. They'll kill me too!"

"What was that?" demanded Trout as he felt a horripilation creeping over him.

The three looked around and at each other silently, questioningly —fearfully.

Blatchly was the first to break the spell. "Keerrrr . . . iiisst!" he exploded. "It almost had me scared too. It's only that bum, Week-end Martin. We've got him locked up in that cell down there. He's getting over one of his jags. It's the first time we've had him in for over two months. I forgot all about him."

Cusani exhaled a breath of relief and pointed to the dead gang-ster. "What do you know about this, Joe?"

"Nothing, Sergeant. Not a thing. Honest . . . When I came down here to talk to him . . . he . . . he . . . was . . . as he is now. You don't think I killed him, do you? . . . I never even touched him . . . You gotta believe me. That Doc Mansfield thinks I did it . . . He didn't say so, but I know from the way he looked at me . . . You know I wouldn't do nothing like that, Sally . . . Don't go back on me now."

"Shut up, damn you!" exclaimed the exasperated Cusani. "We're going to the Chief's office and you come along too. I don't know a thing about this yet, except that you are acting like an idiot. Come on, Major, let's get away from this place or I'll get the jitters too."

He led the way out of the corridor and after leaving instructions not to release Martin, knocked at the Chief's door.

When they had arranged themselves in Donovan's room, Cusani said, "I understand how you feel about this Chief, and the reflection against the department falls on me too, so the sooner we can straighten this out, the better for all of us. From what Joe says, I presume that it was he that found the body. Before we hear his story, I would like to have you tell me what you know so that I'll be up to date and able to follow along with you."

"That's right, Sally," commended Donovan. "That's the orderly way to do it. When I left you at Redfield's, I went and had my din-ner. After that I talked to the Mayor. When I came down here, there were some folks waiting to see me. I had an appointment with Presi-dent Davenport about the commencement arrangements. He came in before I did. He stayed about ten minutes. The other people were a salesman from an auto company about the new scout cars and a lady who wanted to interest me in some racket she had for a police department minstrel show. When I got rid of them, I called up the Fernaud house to see how you were making out with the Redfield case and Sam Lucas told me that you had left there with Professor Trout. I was about to go up to the radio room; they were having some trouble with the new transmitter, when Joe came rushing in and told me that Romano was killed. That was at exactly two o'clock."

"Thank you, Chief. I suppose you asked the Desk Sergeant if any strangers have been around?"

"Yes. It was Lonergan. Shall I tell him to come in?"

"Please."

When Lonergan came in, Cusani took up the inquiry.

"Who has been past the desk that you can remember, since noon, Fred?"

"Well, I came on at twelve and Tom Clancy went home to dinner. Then Sam Fisher took some dinner to the prisoners in the cells and came out and said would I watch the door to the corridor as he wanted to get a bite himself. I can see any one coming in or out from the desk. Blatchly came out of the detective's room and went to see Romano, the guy that was bumped. When he came back he said the punk wouldn't talk but he could make him only the Chief wouldn't let him. He said that he knew a new way some guy from New York had told him. We laughed at him and he went back into the detective's room kind of sore."

They looked at the unhappy Blatchly squirming in his chair, but Cusani ignored him and continued to question Lonergan.

"What else did Joe say?"

"He said you were trying to find out who Romano saw when he was hiding behind the door the time Judge Somers was killed. He said Romano wouldn't tell, but that he could find out."

"I see . . . You said, 'We laughed at him.' Who do you mean by 'We'?"

"Well, there was a lot of the squad there. The relief had just come in and some of them were hanging around."

"Any one else, Fred? Any strangers?"

"Yes, there was that President Davenport of the college. He said that he had a date with the Chief and there was a young fellow who came in about the new cars and there was that fat dame about some benefit she wanted to get up."

"Any one else?"

"No. I guess that's all, Sally. The Chief came in and took Davenport into his office. He stayed there about ten minutes maybe. When he came out he asked me where the can was; he didn't call it that, but I knew what he meant."

"Did you see him come out?"

"No. He must have come out when I was showing that big dame into the office here."

"What time was that?"

"I'd say around one or a little after. Say one ten."

"Who else went into the wash-room?"

"Gosh, Sally, I don't know. Some of the men was going in and out all the time. You know how it is."

"Who else is in the lock-up?"

"Only Week-end Martin, the drunk. We sent the others up to the county jail this morning, but held Romano because Joe said you wanted to talk to him. That's right, isn't it, Joe?"

Blatchly nodded miserably.

"Is there anything you want to ask, Major?" inquired Cusani.

Trout shook his head.

"Okay, Fred. That's all. Send Fisher in."

"Say, Sarge, let me explain," whined Blatchly as Lonergan departed.

"That will wait," replied Cusani. "I want everything in order; you'll get your chance."

Fisher arrived and Sally took up the interrogation.

"When you went in to feed the prisoners did you notice what time it was?"

"Yes, it was 12:10. I had some nice beef-stew and crackers sent in from Gus's and took it in to them. They didn't eat much and I went out home for my own dinner. I got back at 1:15."

"All right. Did you see anybody or anything that might have any bearing on this killing?"

"No. I don't think so, Sergeant. Joe Blatchly went into the corridor as I came out from feeding them and about three-quarters of an hour after I got back, he went in again, but came running out right away and said the guy was croaked."

"Any questions, Major?"

"Yes. Who has charge of the keys to the cells when you are out?"

"No one, sir. There's only one, and it fits all ten. It's that big key that's hanging up on a nail by the corridor door."

"So that almost any one going by could have picked it up and used it?"

"Sure, but who would of wanted to go in there? Besides, Sergeant Lonergan and Joe Blatchly could see any one that went past them, couldn't they?"

"Blatchly might have, if his door was open. Lonergan, however, could not see from where he was sitting at his desk, whether those that passed him went into the washroom or the cell corridor. I am inclined to doubt if Blatchly could either, even if his door was open."

"Why?" asked Cusani.

"I will tell you later. I am not certain yet," answered Trout.

"All right. That's all, Fisher. Bring in Martin."

When Martin entered he proved to be a diminutive, shrivelled, middle-aged man in wrinkled clothes, which, despite their condition, proclaimed loudly their fine quality and excellent tailoring.

He drew himself up stiffly at the door and gazed with an air of hauteur at the occupants of the room. He glanced from one to the other and asked in a soft cultured voice:

"And who is to be Tonas de Torquemada? Not you, my dear Percival, I hope."

Trout, who had been staring amazed at the little man from the moment he entered, gasped, "Good Heavens! Dick Martin."

"Nay, Richard is not himself, Percival. I am simply 'Week-end' Martin, well-known to the Bastiles of Bridgeport, Hartford, Providence and way stations, at your service, gentlemen."

"But Dick, I thought that—"

"Oh yes, I know; my loving family sent me to a private place in Westport and when I escaped from there, to the public institution at Norwich. I am afraid that I am an incorrigible ingrate. However, that has no interest for you."

He looked about him with heavy-lidded, blood-shot eyes and lifted his thin nose as if he had been assailed with something offensive.

"I see," he said, "that the sanctimonious prig, Somers, has gone to his just reward. Suicide, I expect ... Eh? I came on the train with him from New York, Thursday morning and told him a few things for his own good. His damn exquisite conscience must have pricked him a lot. Well, what do you polizei want with me? I am in a hurry. You've kept me longer than you should anyway. I am sailing for France tonight at midnight ... Here is my reservation ... Look at it, Cossacks ... My luggage is down at the pier in New York where my man is probably waiting for me already ... I won't bother you gendarmes again in a hurry. I may decide to stay away for good. I know you'll miss me, you dear old bobbies. You constables wouldn't have seen me this week except that I had an important errand to do in this vicinity. Fire away, coppers. What do you want?"

"Right now," said Cusani, "we want to know anything that you can tell us about what happened in the cell corridor after you had been given your dinner by Officer Fisher."

"After Fisher left, I heard some one go into the other cell and start to badger the chap who was in there but I could not distinguish much. I went to sleep ... When I woke up again, I heard some one ... He was crying ... not loud ... as though he was frightened ... tremulously ... 'I won't talk' ... 'I tell you I won't talk' ... It wasn't loud. It was as though he didn't want to be overheard ... secret. Then there was a growl ... Some one made guttural, threatening sounds ... Then a ... a squeal like a rat caught in a trap ... and a thud and groan. Then a number of squashy noises ... They sounded like ... I don't know how I got the impression, but they sounded like ... like some one throwing fruit and vegetables against a wall ... tomatoes, oranges, pumpkins. There was something horribly nasty about it ... obscene ... ulcerous. Then everything was still. I was frightened ... I heard some one come sneaking up to my cell .. furtively, stealthily ... I feigned sleep as the unholy footsteps stopped at my cell door. I felt as if my life was hanging by a thread. I did not dare to move as I sensed his eyes boring at me ...

lying there . . . helpless. It was a hideous moment and then I heard him whisper softly . . . Oh so softly . . . 'Martin, Martin . . . Are you awake?' . . . I repressed a shudder, but remained quiet. I knew that my life depended on it. After what seemed to me an eternity, I heard him sigh and turn back quietly down the corridor.

"I must have fainted away after that due to my condition, for when I came to, I heard several people talking and gathered that some one had been killed brutally, I called for help, but no one came. That's all I know."

"Did you get a glimpse at the man who looked at you?" asked Cusani after a long pause.

"No, I did not dare to open my eyes. I have absolutely no idea who it was."

"Did you recognize the voice?"

"No."

"Could you tell whether it was a cultured voice or not?"

"No."

"Had you ever heard it before?"

"No. For God's sake, let me alone. I want to forget it."

Cusani looked at him thoughtfully. He saw that Martin was near the edge of a complete breakdown as he stood there twitching. Turning to Trout, he asked, "Is there anything you would like to ask him, Major?"

"Not about this afternoon," answered Trout, "but I would like to know more about his talk with Judge Somers."

Martin drew himself together and said coldly, "That was entirely personal and can have no possible interest to you, Percival."

Constant questioning could elict nothing further and Martin finally became hysterical and shrieked out charges of police persecution and threatened to expose the third degree methods employed, which, he said, had resulted in the death of his fellow prisoner.

Donovan, in a panic, ordered his immediate discharge and Martin, with a leer at Trout, went out with a parting injunction.

"Take care of yourself, Percival, and if you see the virtuous Bill Mather, give him my blessings. He will appreciate them, I know."

Trout, when Martin had gone, explained to the others.

"Martin was a classmate of Somers, in fact, we saw a great deal of him. He was a brilliant scholar, but even then, he showed promise of what he evidently has turned out to be. The last I heard about him was that he had been confined to an institution for inebriates. Funny that he should turn up at this time."

"Why funny, Major?" asked Cusani.

"Well, it seems odd that he should be talking to Somers a few hours before the Judge was killed and also was in town at the time. I wonder what they were talking about on the train."

"If you think that it had anything to do with the murders, it isn't too late to pick him up again."

"No, Sally," said Donovan nervously. "Let him go. We have enough troubles without bringing that bum into this. He can't possibly know anything. He wasn't anywhere near the college when the Judge was killed and we had him locked up tight here when Redfield and Romano were croaked."

"That's true enough, Chief," answered Cusani. "But he knows something. He was one of the last persons to talk to the Judge. He's in it somehow. I'm going to bring him back. I'll take all the responsibility."

He rushed out of the room.

"My God, Prof. Trout. That's going to spill the beans," said Donovan. "Martin may be a bum all right, but his family is one of the most powerful in the state. I might as well give up my job now. He couldn't have done those killings. I can't see why, Sally . . ." He turned to look at Blatchly.

"Joe . . . Are you sure that Martin's cell door was locked? He couldn't have got out, could he?"

"No, Chief, he was locked up tight."

"Do you think he was the killer, Dr. Trout?"

"I don't know. I do think, however, that Sergeant Cusani is right to hold him. First, because he undoubtedly knows something important, and secondly, because that knowledge is dangerous. We have had two murders already for that reason. Martin should unquestionably be locked up for his own good and a strict watch kept over him."

Cusani entered with Martin. The little man was beside himself with helpless rage.

"Why? . . . Why? . . . Why?" he sputtered. "You'll sweat for this. All of you . . . You, Percy, you filthy cad. You don't think that I murdered that whited sepulchre, Somers, do you? Much as he deserved killing!"

"I am not in charge here, Martin," said Trout kindly. "Chief Donovan has reconsidered his decision and believes that you should tell us what you and Somers talked about on the train."

"I told you that that was personal. No one who lays claim to being a gentleman would want to stick his nose into a personal matter."

"Okay," said Cusani. "I am not a gentleman. So go ahead; tell me all about it."

"You don't have to tell me that you are no gentleman. Neither is Trout, if it comes to that, nor is he," said Martin, pointing to the worried Donovan. "You are all a lot of muckers and you can't scare me."

Trout rose and said, "If my being present, Martin, embarrasses you, I'll leave and you can talk to the Chief and Sergeant Cusani privately. They are only doing their duty in trying to solve a murder."

"Don't be such a damn hypocrite, Trout. You know damn well that Mather knows all about it. Why don't you ask him instead of baiting me? Or if it comes to that, why don't you speak up yourself?"

"I don't know what you're talking about," said Trout bluntly. Martin sneered. "Somers, Martin and Trout . . . The Holy Trinity." He pointed an accusing finger at the indignant Major. "And you stand there and say that you don't know what I am talking about. Well, Somers knew and he is dead. I know that Mathers knows and I'm willing to bet what is left of my inheritance, that you know too."

"Well, I don't, and if you know anything, you ought to tell us now for your own protection. You heard a man being murdered in his cell today. That man was killed because he knew too much. We had just left the scene of another murder. That man was also killed because he knew too much. First Somers, then Redfield, then Rom . . ."

"Redfield? You say Redfield?" Martin shrank back. "No . . . No . . . Redfield. My God, Percy, there's a ghastly mistake here . . . I am all wrong . . . I don't know anything . . . I . . . I . . . Redfield."

He stopped and pulled himself together with an effort. "But, after all, it may be only a coincidence in names. Who in Hell is Redfield?"

"He was a campus guard and . . . Bert Somers' son."

"And he was murdered? Are you sure?" whispered Martin.

"Yes, Dick. He was murdered."

"It's insanity!" cried the terror-stricken Martin. "It can't be. It's a horrible blunder. It's . . . Was Redfield living here in town all the time?"

"For the past three years anyway," answered Trout.

"Did he? . . ." Martin hesitated. "Did he know he was Somers' son?"

"We don't know whether he did or not, Dick. Mather does not think so."

"But Mather knew that Redfield was the son?"

"Yes."

Martin looked searchingly at Trout, then turned to Donovan and said, "Chief Donovan, please accept my apology for talking to you the way I did. You were right in wanting to protect me. I want to be taken to the county jail and locked up with a trustworthy guard placed over me."

Cusani peered curiously at the little man. "We will protect you all right, Mr. Martin," he said. "But you haven't told us anything yet."

"And I'm not going to. It's too dangerous to do any talking . . . I don't know whom to trust . . . Anyway, I don't know anything. I . . . I was mistaken . . . I am asking for protection. Do I get it?

If you won't give it to me, the Governor of the State will. I am not talking because I don't know anything about this rotten business. I thought I did, but I was mistaken."

"Well," said Cusani. "You know what you said to Judge Somers on the train. Don't you?"

"Yes."

"Tell us that anyway," persisted Cusani.

"I only told him that the girl he had ruined was dead. She had died in France. He already had been told about it, it seems."

"So you knew all about her," said Sally. "Who was she?"

"She went by the name of Madam Redfield. That's all I know. You evidently know as much about it as I do."

"If that is the case," remarked Cusani, "why do you want protection?"

"Because a mistake has been made . . . and I . . . and it may happen again . . . That's all I know. Now, do I get that protection, or do I have to go to the Governor, who is a friend of the family?"

"No. You won't have to that, Mr. Martin," said Donovan placatingly. "I'll arrange it for you myself. Come along with me now. You can talk with him later, Sally. Come with me Mr. Martin."

"Not alone. Not with you or anyone else alone."

Chief Donovan frowned. "Why not, Mr. Martin?"

"You don't get me alone. I don't trust you."

"Well, whom do you trust?"

"Not a soul now."

"But that's ridiculous," said Trout. "Chief Donovan is only trying to help you."

"Ridiculous is it? You'd better watch your own step, Percy. Bill Mather, too . . . There's Hell waiting around the corner for you all."

"Look here, Martin," snapped out Cusani. "You either know something that we should know, or you are still drunk."

"I don't know a thing that you don't know already. Trout says that two men have been murdered for knowing too much. I don't know how much they knew. Perhaps they knew more than I do perhaps not. I . . . Well, I don't know anything."

"What do you want me to do?" asked the confused Chief.

"I want two of the guards from the county jail to come down here and fetch me and lock me up and guard me while I am there with instructions to allow no one to see me without my permission. That's what I want. Do I get it?"

Cusani snorted at such a fantastic request, but Donovan, anxious to placate, said, "I can arrange it. Come on out to the desk with me and I'll fix it up for you."

They walked out together.

"What do you think of that? Is he still drunk?" asked Cusani.

"No, Sally, I don't think so. You must remember that he has been through a harrowing experience. That was a strange reaction when he heard that Redfield was killed though."

"What did he mean when he warned us?"

"I don't know."

"Ah," broke in Blatchly, who had been silent for an unusually long time. "The Chief's too easy."

"Hold your trap, Joe," barked Cusani. "You're not out of the woods yet by a damn sight."

Donovan returned smiling. "Well, I fixed that up. He's out there on the bench talking with Fred and Tom. The sheriff is sending two men down for him. He's a harmless little fellow after all."

"As harmless as a rattlesnake," murmured Trout.

"What did you say, Major?"

"Nothing, Chief. I've been thinking about Martin and somehow I can't get it out of my mind that he is responsible for this whole thing. While he didn't do the actual killing, he started it on its way. I don't mean that he conspired with the killer or anything like that. What I do mean is that he was the torch. If he had not come to town Thursday, the murders would not have taken place."

"How do you make that out?" asked Cusani.

"It stands to reason. He talked to Somers on the train and admitted to us that he knew something . . . I don't like it."

"Yes, Major. He also said that you and Mather knew the same thing," said Cusani, as he eyed Trout searchingly.

Trout smiled wearily. "Yet, Sally, I haven't any idea what he meant, unless I have entirely misread the data we have collected."

"Okay," said Cusani. "Let's get everything in order and see where we stand."

CHAPTER 16

SERGEANT CUSANI turned to Blatchly and said, "And now, Joe, I guess we are ready to hear your story."

"All right, and I'm damn glad to get it off my chest. I'll start at the beginning so that you'll have everything straight. When the Chief and the others went out to Redfield's, they left me here all alone except the regulars like Sergeant Clancy and Fisher. I took care of the routine reports and talked a while to some reporters. I didn't tell them nothing . . . Merely kidded them along. Some one tipped them off to the Redfield conk and they all beat it in a hurry. I waited around for somebody to come and relieve me, so that I could go and get some eats. But you was all too busy, I guess, to think of me, so I goes down to try to get that Romano to loosen up. He wasn't talking. Honest, Chief, I didn't lay a finger on him. I kept asking him who the guy was that he saw until my tongue was hanging out. I couldn't get a rise out of him. I went back and talked to Sergeant Lonergan and the boys for a few minutes, like he told you and then went back to the detectives' room. I was pretty tired, so I laid down and got a little rest. About two o'clock, I went down to see Romano again . . . It was too late . . . He was beat up . . . He was croaked."

Cusani said to Trout, "What do you think of his story, Major? Sounds pretty thin to me."

"No, Sally, I think that Joe is telling the truth. In fact, I do not see how he could have done the killing himself. I believe that he was responsible for Romano's death, but entirely unwittingly."

"How do you deduce that?" asked Cusani as Blatchly and Donovan leaned back with sighs of relief.

"In the first place," said Trout, "Blatchly could have known nothing of the Romano murder because when it happened, he was probably asleep. When we arrived on the scene, he was in his shirt-sleeves. As I went past his room I noticed that his coat was folded at the head of the couch in there as if it had been used for a pillow. Now he has his coat on again, and I have been looking at it carefully while he has been sitting here. He could not have been the killer . . . Wait a minute until I have finished. That killing was a particularly gory one. Blatchly's white shirt was clean; his hands were clean, and his coat was clean, nor was there any sign of effort having been made to remove bloodstains from any of them. From the condition of that cell, it was manifestly impossible for the murderer to have escaped being bespattered with blood.

"Let me tell you what I think actually took place. This man was wearing a suit of dark clothes which would not show damp spots readily. He stepped into the wash-room at the corridor door, washed his hands and wiped off his clothes with a wet towel and walked out. If you go to the wash-room now, you will probably find some blood-soaked towels hidden there."

Cusani and Blatchly rushed out and returned shortly with a half a dozen towels, smeared with drying blood.

"You were right, Major. We found them shoved down in the bottom of the soiled towel receptacle. This fellow, whoever it is, must be a pretty cool customer. Imagine going in there and calmly washing himself. Why almost any one could have walked in and caught him at it."

"Yes," retorted Trout, "and some one may have seen him, but did not know what he was doing. Lonergan said there were several persons going in and out of there; policemen and others."

"Gosh, how about President Davenport?"

"I was wondering when you would think of him, Sally. Chief Donovan, I would suggest that you detail two of your best men to keep a watch over President Davenport."

"But, Professor, you don't think that he did it, do you?"

"I am not taking any more chances on sudden deaths. I would like to have him guarded and his house watched, night and day. If there is any complaint, I will take the responsibility. By not taking the precautions which common sense should have dictated to me, we have permitted this murderer to run riot. I can only blame myself that these two additional crimes have been committed. I should have foreseen them both."

He looked around gloomily and added, "Perhaps you'd better do the same for Dean Mather."

Donovan acceded readily to these requests. Here was something that he could understand; some one needed to be watched. He stepped out of the room and gave the necessary orders and saw that they were carried out. He felt that at last he was doing something. When he returned he had regained some of his equanimity. "Well, that's done," he said, importantly. "What next?"

Cusani looked up at his Chief and said, "The next thing is that I want your permission to demote Blatchly."

"Demote Joe Blatchly? But why, Sally?"

"For several reasons. First, for sleeping when he should have been on watch, and secondly, for talking too damn much. I know now what Major Trout meant when he said that Blatchly was unwittingly responsible for Romano's death."

"I guess you're right. I hate to do it, Joe, but Sally is right. You can report to Cap. Shultz over in the Second, for duty. Get back in uniform and go up there tonight. Perhaps some walking on the pavements would do you good."

When Blatchly had gone, Donovan asked, "What next, Sally?"

Cusani looked inquiringly at Trout, who was making notes on some papers which he had taken from his pocket. When he finished, he looked up and said, "I think that the best way to make any orderly progress is to check up everything that we know and arrange it on some sort of sequence. We haven't finished yet with all the collected data on the Judge's death. These murders remind me somewhat of the large pancakes my fishing guide in Maine makes. You haven't finished one, before he slides another fresh one onto your plate. Let's go back to the first murder. Who were our suspects? Redfield, Romano, and Sally has added Mather. Redfield and Romano are dead. That leaves Mather. I think that we are agreed that only one person committed all three murders. If that is so, we can eliminate Mather also. While it was possible for him to have done either of the first two, it was not possible for him to have done the third, as he was with us at the time it was done. That is, between twelve thirty and two this afternoon. Is that agreed?"

Chief Donovan assented readily, but Cusani pondered over the question. "Don't think that I am trying to raise foolish objections, but what proof have we that one person and only one, did the three killings?"

"No proof; but we must use our reasoning. Either one person or a gang did them. I have no room in my mind for any hypothesis that would admit of such a fantastic series of coincidences. The three victims made unusual contact Thursday afternoon. Today, Monday, all three have been killed. If they had been in the habit of meeting, even occasionally, I might admit of a chance of coincidence in their deaths, but when the three murders followed after contacts which were very unusual, to say the least, there can be no doubt as to their relation. The three murders are tied together and we must accept that as a working basis for the solution. If any inconsistencies should upset this theory as we proceed, we can apply the principles of inductive philosophy and I will gladly change our line. After all reasoning, when compared to logical argumentation, is more or less informal. Do you agree?"

"Sure, that's right," acceded Donovan. "Let's keep it all free and easy. I never did like those formal affairs," and suiting his actions to words, he removed his coat and loosened his collar.

"All right, then," said Trout hurriedly, as Cusani looked doubtfully at his Chief, "here is a sketch I have made of Somers' room. I want you to bear in mind carefully all the details that I have shown on it. Now we will take those data that we have and apply to them

A—Where Mather found hat

B—2nd position of hat

X—Where bullet struck

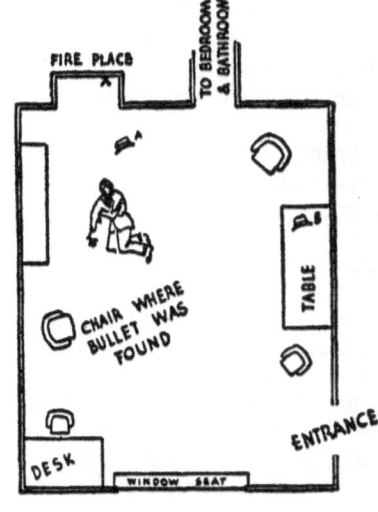

our evidence and deductive reasoning. I have checked and rechecked
the time-table and it cannot be wrong. The first visitor was Redfield.
He came in and took off his hat respectfully, if not politely, and
placed it on the table. Young Somers' hat was lying there also. Redfield's business with the Judge was concluded quickly and probably
in a friendly spirit. He left in haste . . . He had a short time only in
which to meet the man from the finance company . . . He picked up
the wrong hat. When he left, Somers was still living. Our proof for
all that is contained in Redfield's statement, substantiated by Romano and young Somers, also by the hat which made its final ap-
pearance in President Davenport's possession. Redfield, therefore,
was not the killer. Do you agree?"

Donovan and Cusani nodded.

Trout continued, "Romano was the next. He went in . . . Demanded a release for his brother . . . Had a scuffle . . . Lost his gun,
which was discharged during the fight . . . Was hit in the eye and
kicked out. When he left, Somers was still living. Our proofs are
the finger-prints on the gun, the bullet in the chair which matched
the rifling, the cut under his eye, the gun itself in Somers' pocket,
and Romano's own statement. Do you agree?"

"Sure," said Donovan.

Cusani, however, interposed an objection. "How do you know that
the Judge was still alive? What was to prevent Romano from pull-
ing another gun and drilling him, picking up the bullet and running
out? How do we know that his whole statement isn't false?"

"That's where the ring comes in, Sally."

"Do you mean the Judge's ring that I had the laboratory test
made on for blood?"

"Exactly. When Somers hit Romano, he cut the gangster's face
with the ring. After Romano went out, Somers went into the bathroom to wash his hands and clean the ring. Therefore, he was still
alive after Romano had left. Is that clear now?"

Cusani nodded his agreement.

"All right, then. Let me try to reconstruct the final scene in this
act. The killer tiptoes in . . . there is no one in the room . . . Somers
is in the bath-room washing . . . The killer walks across the room
and announces his presence . . . Perhaps calls out to Somers. He
may have heard the water running in the wash bowl . . . Somers
comes into the door . . . Sees a man facing him with a revolver . . .
Rushes at him as he did at Romano and is shot dead. The bullet
passes through him and strikes the back of the fireplace, bounds
back and passes through the hat which is lying on the floor where
it had fallen during the struggle over the gun with Romano. The
killer picks up the bullet, which has spent itself, pockets his gun
and walks out. I can't see how it could have happened any other
way. The hat lying on the table where Mather had placed it, con-

fused me for a time. If you will refer to the sketch of the room, you will note that it would have been impossible for the bullet to ricochet from the back of the fireplace to the hat on the table. The fireplace is too deep. Mather, however, cleared that up for us. How does that strike you?"

"That's a very reasonable explanation, Major, and I would accept it, except that it has a serious flaw," said the Sergeant.

"What is it? That's what we are here for," piped Trout.

"You haven't eliminated Mather yet. Suppose Romano's story of the third man is nothing but a lot of hooey. We have no proof that it wasn't. How do you account for the missing rifle? No, Major, you haven't cleared Mather yet."

"Oh, but I have, Sally. I will admit that at one time, when there seemed to be many clues pointing at him, I had a fleeting suspicion and I did a damn fool thing, but now I know that it was impossible for Bill Mather to have shot Somers from his rooms across the campus."

"Why?"

"Look at the plan of the room. For the bullet to enter the room through the window, pass through Somers' body and hit the back of the fireplace, it must have gone through the curtain hanging at the north end of the window. I examined that curtain and it was not torn. Another reason which makes it impossible is that Mather's rooms, like mine, are on the ground floor. The fireplace in Somers' room is high and the bullet struck high, but not high enough if it was fired from Mather's rifle on the ground floor. I am sufficiently versed in ballistics to know that that rifle of Mather's has a flat trajectory at at least three hundred yards and it is only two hundred yards across the campus. It would have lodged itself above the mantel-shelf. The same reasoning would also exclude any stray shot that may have come from the campus. Those bullets would have struck the ceiling. I think that our best reason, however, for eliminating Mather, outside of his character and the devotion he felt for Somers, is the fact that these crimes are closely related and the acts of one man."

"Okay, Major, I am convinced. How does that leave us now?"

"That we must postulate the third man and accept Romano's unsupported word. I don't for a minute doubt the truth of his statement . . . His death proves it. He was killed because he recognized the murderer and because Blatchly talked too much."

"I think that's so. What have we that will lead us to this third man?" asked Cusani.

"Not much yet, but I am collecting a little here and a little there, and I may be able to identify him soon. I am not ready to tell you anything definite yet, not even to make a guess, but I have my ideas. Now, unless you or the Chief would like to add anything to what we already have discussed about the first killing, I think that we should take up the Redfield case and straighten that out as well as we can."

Trout turned to Donovan and explained. "You understand, Chief, that there are many details which we are omitting from this summary. As a matter of fact, about all we are doing now is to get the necessary 'where, when and how' co-ordinated . . . separate the chaff from the wheat if we can, otherwise we would soon find ourselves in a mess. There are so many false clues taking up our time which we should be devoting to essentials."

Donovan bowed importantly. "You are quite right, Professor."

"What do you say, Sally?"

"Of course you are right, but before we leave the first case, what about that missing rifle?"

"That was where I made a fool of myself," admitted Trout. "When Mather went to New York, I slipped into his room and took it. It is in the closet of my room. It was a silly thing to do."

Cusani smiled and said, "I thought that you had something to do with it. You seemed to know quite a lot about it. Well, I guess that clears up all my objections and we can go ahead with Redfield now. Perhaps I'd better tell the story as I was the first on the scene. You can check me up as I go along, Major."

He lighted a fresh cigarette, and after a few moments of concentration, began. "I picked up your short wave signal in my car, Chief, and beat it over to Redfield's as quick as I could. The alarm went out at 11:47. It didn't take me more than three minutes to get there."

"Wait a minute," interrupted Trout, and turned to Donovan, who was lighting a cigar. "May I have one of your cigars, Chief? Thanks. Go ahead, Sally."

"When I got there the first person I saw was Miss Fernaud. She was terribly excited and grabbed hold of me. She kept saying that the police had killed Redfield. Then you all came in. Now in this case we have only one suspect, the man that Redfield himself let into the house. It would be unreasonable to suspect Miss Elsie, and, although there is a direct accusation against the police, I think that we can bar that out also. Then there is the man that that big cow, Thelma, saw driving off. Who was he? Was he the man that Redfield admitted? What was he doing there at that time? He drove off at 10:30. What was he doing in a car that looked like one of our cruisers, or like the car that Mather admitted he was using? . . . Hell, Major, you may have cleared the Dean of the first murder, but how are you going to whitewash him this time?"

"Well, I think that I can do that, too . . . If Redfield made an engagement to meet any one so early in the morning, that engagement was probably made the day before; that is, yesterday. Yesterday Mather was in New York, and it is most unlikely that any such tryst was made then. We can check that with Miss Fernaud. She may have heard something . . . Perhaps a telephone conversation."

"I don't think that's a very hot argument, Major. He might . . ."

"Yes, I know. He may have done many things, but I am not depending on any spurious arguments to clear Mather. The man who was seen going away in the car was wearing a uniform and a badge of some sort. What would Mather be doing in such a masquerade? No one who had just committed a murder would advertise the fact by slamming a door as he was leaving the scene of the crime. Not our killer, anyway, for we have proof that he was stealthy and silent. The man we want is a cigar-smoker. Mather never smokes cigars . . . Speaking of cigars, will you please produce that butt you took from Redfield's room? Chief Donovan and I have been conducting a little experiment which I would like to put to test now. Will you please let me have the cigar that you are smoking, Chief?"

The puzzled Chief handed Trout his partly consumed cigar and Cusani produced the stub. Trout laid them side by side on the glass-topped table and added his own. He reached into his pocket and took out an envelope and shook out its contents beside the three cigars; a paper match folder and four burnt matches.

"Here's where I am going to do some deducing, as Sally would say. You will notice that these three cigars are of the same brand. A brand manufactured right here in this city and very popular here, although little known out of town. You will also note that the three stubs are nearly of the same size. The one that I smoked is a little shorter than the others, while the Chief's is slightly longer than the one we found on the floor of Redfield's room. We know that Redfield was not a cigar smoker. I do not think that there can be any doubt but that that cigar was smoked by Redfield's visitor. I smoke cigarettes and I have noticed that a person who smokes them is a faster smoker than one who smokes cigars.

"I timed myself and the Chief from the moment we lighted our cigars and I find that it took us exactly twenty minutes to reduce them to their present size. Thelma told us that the caller arrived at nine-thirty. He was there when Elsie returned from her marketing at nine-forty-five. I believe that I can place the time of the murder at not much later than ten o'clock and as the murderer would make his escape as soon as possible, we may assume that Redfield was attacked and the killer out of the house, a full half hour before the door was slammed."

"Hold on there, Major. You are way ahead of me. How do you deduce all that?" cried the astonished Sergeant.

"I admit that it is rather tricky, but I am sure that I am right," said Trout with a smile. "It's a match trick. The ordinary match folder contains twenty paper matches. This one, which I picked up in Redfield's room is different. As you see, it is one of those with printing on the matches themselves. The matches are wider and flatter. It held twelve matches originally, in two layers of six each. There are eight in it now. Those four loose ones are the ones which came out of it. The legend on both layers is the same,

COUNTY

GARAGE

two letters on each match. On the first match the letters C and G; the C above the G. On the second, O and A and so forth. The six matches on the back sheet are exactly the same as those immediately in front of them. The ones that were torn out and used were the first four, two front and two back. Three of these were used to light cigarettes and one to light a cigar. The one to light the cigar was the first match out of the folder ... All right, Sally. Wait until I have finished. I think I can answer all of your objections ... When a cigarette is lighted, in most cases only the head of the match is burned. The lighting of a cigar is usually a much more deliberate process and the match is well burned down before the smoker is satisfied with his light. You will note that one match and only one is burned lower than the head. That will also eliminate the possibility of the cigar having become extinguished and relighted and in that way interfere with our time measure."

"Anyway," interposed Cusani, "there were only four matches; one for the cigar and the others for the three cigarettes."

"That is true, but one may raise the point that Redfield could have lighted one cigarette from the glowing end of another. Remember he lit three cigarettes in a comparatively short time. To light a cigar that has already gone out once, usually takes longer than to get the first light. So we can forget that. Is that all clear now?"

"Yes, that part is, but I don't follow you when you say that the cigar match was the first one. I can see that it was one of the C and G ones, but it does not follow that it was the one on the front sheet. It could have been the second or even the third."

"That is where you insult my intelligence, Sally. You don't think that I would overlook that, would you? Before you joined us in my rooms after we had left Redfield's, I made several tests. Look here ... I'll show you."

He picked up the folder.

"See ... The tops of these matches are even. Now, if you try to replace the C and G match that was used on the cigarette into the front sheet, it will be too short; but try it on the back sheet and it will just fit. Therefore, the one that was used on the cigar came from the front sheet and was the first match to be used. Right?"

Cusani nodded, while the Chief held his head in bewilderment. "It is interesting to note," continued Trout, "that in most cases the matches that are torn from the back sheets are usually broken shorter than those taken from the front. Try it some time. This time, however, we were fortunate to have the folder itself, and we could fit them in their proper places. We may, therefore, be positive."

"That's all very clever, Major," said Cusani, "but what does it get us?"

"A great deal. I can place the time of the assault within fifteen minutes and eliminate some more false clues . . . When Elsie returned at 9:45, she told us that she smelled tobacco smoke in the hall. If we allow two minutes for the smoke to have reached the hall from the room, the latest for the cigar to have been lighted would have to be 9:43. It took him twenty minutes to smoke it down to the size in which we found it. That would make it 10:03 or earlier when Redfield was hit."

"Suppose that the cigar had gone out and was not relit say, twenty minutes before he hit him, where would your fine theory be then?" asked Cusani.

"But it didn't, Didymus. It didn't, and you ought to know it didn't."

"Sure . . . I remember now that when I picked it up, it had burned a hole in the rug." He grinned boyishly, and added, "I don't mind you calling me names that I can understand, Major, but what in hell is a 'diddle-mouse'? Should I pull my gun and say 'Smile, damn you, when you call me that'?"

"No, you chump. It's only another way of saying that you come from Missouri."

"All right," said Sally, "let's get going. What else do you deduce, Major?"

"That the murderer is a local man, that he wears dark clothes, that he is strong and agile and can move swiftly and silently. That he knew Redfield and maybe Romano too before he committed the first murder and that we all know him, or at least, have seen him ourselves. He smokes cigars and is fearless."

"Well, that's a lot more than I expected. I can follow you through most of it, but why do you think he is a local?"

"On account of his familiarity with the locale. He was also smoking a local brand of cigar with which a stranger would not be familiar."

"That doesn't follow. Redfield might have given it to him."

"Not likely, Sally; there were no other cigars there and that brand sells at three for a quarter. I can't see Redfield buying a single cigar for his visitor. Can you?"

"Well, he might have given him all three, or he might have had just one left from some he had bought at some other time."

"That is possible, but not probable. The cigar was not an old one. It was quite fresh and it is most unlikely that Redfield would give a caller three cigars at one time . . . Too much like saying, 'Here old man, I spent a quarter on you for these cigars. I don't smoke them myself. Take them all.' When we called on him Saturday, Miss Fernaud offered us cigarettes. If there had been cigars there, he or she would have offered them."

"I guess you're right, Major. Perhaps I am getting too technical. We'd better stick to probabilities. Do you think it is probable that Redfield smoked three cigarettes in twenty minutes?"

"He didn't. He lighted three but smoked only two. He had just lighted the third when he was hit. It was not lying among the ashes and debris from the smoking stand, but was off the rug, on the hardwood floor, where it had burned itself out. It was almost entire. The cigar butt, however, was with the other articles and that helps me to reconstruct the act. Would you like to hear how I think it was done?"

"Yes, Professor Trout, we sure would," said Donovan heartily. Cusani merely nodded.

"Mind you, I can't prove this, but I think that you will agree that it is correct. They sat opposite each other with the smoking stand between them. The killer leaned forward several times to knock the ashes from his cigar into the tray . . . Redfield was lighting his third cigarette . . . The visitor leaned over again as if to deposit more ashes. Instead of which, he dropped his cigar, sprang to his feet, with the heavy stand in his hands, swung it around, hitting Redfield on the back of the head and hurried out. Redfield's attention was diverted as he was lighting the cigarette . . . The killer closed the room door carefully; but the heavier front door, which was apt to be noisier, he left open. I would place the time at ten o'clock."

Cusani, who had been listening to the summary with rapt attention, nodded and said, "Yes, Major, I agree. That's probably exactly what happened . . . Well, I don't know whether you have considered it, but that also about eliminates all our good suspects."

"We still have Miss Fernaud, but I doubt if she has the strength to swing that heavy stand. Thelma, of course, could do it."

"What for?"

"To protect her virtue."

"How about Martin?"

"I don't see how we can make him fit at all, Sally."

"Neither do I. Now, about this Romano killing . . . It seems to me that the field is narrowed down considerably. There is President Davenport." He stopped and looked at Trout, who frowned and shook his head slowly. "Then, of course, I don't know where Mather was at the time. He and you had left Redfield's together. When I saw him next, he was in your room. It was during that time that Romano was killed. I suppose that you can give him an alibi."

"Certainly. He was with me every moment."

"And you went directly to your room?"

"Yes, Sally," said Trout with a smile. "Yes we did."

"It's getting late," said Cusani abruptly. "Thanks a lot, Major. I've a few things I want to clean up and if you don't mind, I will drop in to see you later. About nine o'clock, okay?"

CHAPTER 17

AT NINE O'CLOCK Cusani and Trout were seated in the latter's room on the campus. Sally was speaking. "There is one thing about Redfield that I can't get out of my mind . . . He reminds me of some one whom I have seen, but I can't place him."

"Somers maybe," suggested Trout.

"No, it's some one else . . . Some one that I have talked to quite recently. I've checked every possible person, but, no dice."

"Too bad, Sally. I know how you feel. It will come to you like 'Mr. Addison Sims of Seattle.' "

"Okay, but it's worrying me. Now let's get everything down that we know and start right. Let's see where we could have slipped up. I am sure we know the man who did it all right, but we can't point the finger to him. It's some one we have mentioned in our summary, but he slips out of our fingers every time, just as we are about to grab him. Let's see, who haven't we cleared yet? Who haven't we eliminated beyond a doubt? . . . Redfield and Romano are dead. Mather was with you when Romano was killed. Somers was in New York. Martin was locked up. I even checked up on old Finn. He was walking his beat when Redfield was killed. Blatchly you yourself eliminated. President Davenport? Where was he? But, of course, that's out. Why should he? Well then, who is left? There's you and me and Chief Donovan; all with perfect alibis." He laughed grimly. "Yes, we have done a swell job in finding out who didn't do it. Now let's find out who did."

They discussed the problem from every angle for three hours.

It was midnight when Trout summed up.

"I believe that we have swept everything clear except the one mysterious figure that runs like a red silk thread through the murky pattern of the whole fabric. We do not know who he is, but, Sally, my boy, I am getting closer and closer to him. A little here and a little there . . . One brick laid on another and a little mortar and the building grows apace. The foundations are laid. The walls are beginning to rise. There are a number of things that I must do and by this time tomorrow night, I will know a great deal more about . . ."

He stopped abruptly and with a sharp warning cry, made a dive at Cusani's knees, bringing him crashing to the floor.

Almost simultaneously, there was a tinkle of breaking glass and a sound like a short cough.

"Wait. Don't get up yet," whispered Trout. "He may be there . . ."

"I hope he is," exclaimed Cusani, struggling free. "This time he won't get away."

He dashed out of the door and out on the campus, closely followed by Trout.

But the campus was deserted under the star-lit sky.

They stood for a moment wrapped in silence . . . The quiet was shattered by the staccato sputtering of an automobile. The noise came through the west portal, about twenty yards away. They raced to the spot and as they turned into the dark mouth of the arch, Trout collided heavily with some one with whom he grappled and went sprawling to the ground.

Cusani rushed out to the street in time to see the lights of a taxi-cab disappearing around the next corner. He jumped into his own car, which was parked at the curb nearby. After several ineffectual attempts to start it and wasting precious minutes, he lifted the hood and found that the battery wires had been deliberately disconnected. He clenched his fists in helpless rage and rushed back to find Trout leaning over a figure seated on the ground with its back propped against the wall.

He drew out his flash-light and asked, "Who is it?"

"Young Bob Somers. I bumped into him and must have knocked him out."

Somers shook his head gingerly and said with a sorry smile, "Not quite, Professor, but I must say that it was a rather rough welcome."

In answer to Cusani's rapid questioning, he told them that he had returned from New York by a late train and had taken a taxi from the station.

"Did you see any one as you arrived here?"

"What's it all about? Why the excitement, Sergeant?"

"Answer me quick," barked out Cusani. "Some one tried to wipe out Trout!"

"Yes," answered Bob hurriedly. "While I was paying my fare, a drunk came up and asked to be taken to the station. Said he wanted to make the 'Owl' to Boston."

"Are you sure he was drunk?"

"Absolutely. I not only could see, but I could smell that he was."

"What did he look like?"

"I didn't notice him particularly. He gave me the impression of being under-sized and not young."

"Come in back to the room. I'm going to do some telephoning. We've got time to catch him yet."

They ran back to the room. Cusani snatched the telephone and was soon talking to the taxi dispatcher at the railroad station giving him instructions to hold the driver and his passenger on their arrival. He also talked to the patrolman on point duty at the same place, to whom he gave Trout's number with an order to call him as soon as the capture was made.

Meanwhile Trout had been inspecting the walls and searching the floor of the room carefully. When Cusani had finished at the 'phone, Trout turned to him.

"I think you are wasting your time on that taxi lead, Sally. It's a wash-out."

"Why?"

"Because the person that went away in the taxi wasn't the one that fired the shot at us. That man returned to this room during our absence."

"What do you mean?"

"Just as I said. He didn't go away in the taxi. While we were wasting our time hunting for him outside, he stepped in here, dug the bullet out of the wall where I saw it as we ran out, and walked calmly away."

Trout pointed out the hole in the wall where the missile had lodged. The bullet had been dug out.

Cusani dashed for the window.

"What are you going to do?" asked Trout.

"What I should have done ten minutes ago." He drew a police whistle from his pocket and blew three shrill blasts into the silent night.

He waited a moment then stepped out of the room into the hall and out onto the campus.

He blew three more calls, long and shrill. This time there were results.

Running footsteps were heard coming from all directions, lights sprang up all around the quadrangle and the section doors began to belch out a noisy multitude.

Hundreds of students in every manner of undress assembled in shouting, jeering groups. Groups were merged into other groups and almost miraculously, a crowd of nearly a thousand young, care-free revelers had gathered.

Some one shouted, "A parade!" Others called for the band.

Cusani stamped back into Trout's room.

"That's torn it," he growled. "How are we going to stop these wild men?"

"I'll show you," said Trout. "Let me have that whistle."

He leaned out of the window and blew three long shrill blasts. In a minute the crowd swarmed about in front of him. He whis-pered something to Bob, who nodded and stepped to the open win-dow.

After he had attracted sufficient attention, he raised his hand for silence. There were a few calls of, "Hi Bob!" "He's going to make a speech," and "Shut up you fellows," but curiosity soon got the best of them and some degree of order obtained.

Like his father, Bob was a natural born leader. His great pop-ularity gave him a tremendous advantage, which the canny Trout had been quick to seize and put to use. He stood with the light from the room shining full upon him . . . His young face grave and sober.

He began to speak. "Fellows, we need your help. A serious crime has been attempted here on the campus tonight. I don't need to re-mind you of what happened here last Thursday. This might have been as serious. It is a case where we must help the police. We can do that best by going quietly to our rooms and not interfering. I also have been asked to get your cooperation in searching for the criminal, who may still be somewhere on the grounds or hiding in one of the buildings. Will you please go to your rooms now and search them carefully. If you see anything that looks suspicious, re-port it here. If not, please stay in your quarters. You will know all about it in the morning. Thank you."

The crowd gave a cheer for Bob, one for "Piping Perce," and another one, in which some of the Bronx variety were mingled, for the police, and dispersed to the dormitories. The whole perform-ance had not taken more than fifteen minutes.

In the meantime the report had come through from the taxi dis-patcher and confirmed Trout's prediction. The passenger was a well-known merchant of the city, who could not have had anything to do with the attempted killing. He was ordered released in time to catch his train.

"Thanks, Bob," said Trout warmly. "That was fine work."

"That's all right, Professor. Unless you want me for anything else, I think that I'll turn in."

When Bob had gone, Trout surveyed those that remained in the room. Dean Mather had entered during the disturbance. He and

Trout were the only faculty members occupying rooms on that quadrangle. They were, to some extent, responsible for the maintenance of discipline in that area. The others in the room, who had come in answer to Cusani's whistle, were four uniformed policemen. Standing out among them, his uniform fitting as snug as the skin on a sausage, was ex-detective Blatchly.

"Well," said Cusani. "Here's our little play-mate again. Good morning, Joe, and what may you be doing here?"

"I reported to Cap. Shultz like the Chief told me. He didn't put me on the beats as the detail was made up already, but he had an order from headquarters for a special detail to watch Dean Mather here, and he sent me and Jim White on it. That's how we got here so quick when you blew your whistle."

"All right. How about you, Maloney? Where were you?"

"I had just come on duty. This is my regular beat. I was talking to Finn, who was going off. He's on the eight to twelve, when we heard your whistle and we both beat it over here as fast as we could."

"That's good," said the Sergeant. "Now I'll tell you what happened. Some one tried to knock off either Major Trout or me. If it hadn't been for the Major's quick thinking, one of us would probably be laid out with a slug in his brain. We both ran out after him . . . We didn't even see him. I got onto a phony trail and we wasted a lot of time. When we got back here, we found that the bullet, which had been sticking in the wall over there when we went out, had been dug out and taken away. It's the same stunt that he pulled in Judge Somers' killing. The murderer was probably in the vicinity when I called. What a lucky break he got then! Of course, he had all kinds of chances to make his get-away with that gang of crazy kids."

"But, Sergeant, we didn't hear no shots," said Blatchly.

"He was using a silencer," explained Cusani. "What I want to know is whether you men saw anything or anybody around here that could have had anything to do with this. You, Finn. Did you see anything?"

"No. I was on my beat. I got on at eight. I seen your car when you came up. That would be about nine. No. Things was quiet all night. I was going off, like Maloney told you, when we hears the whistle. The regerlations says, 'Any officer, no matter if he is on or off duty, when he hears . . . "

"Yes Pat, we know all about it. Did you see any one go near my car?"

"No Sally, I didn't."

The other men, when questioned, could add no further information and Cusani stood up and looked at them thoughtfully.

"I don't know as there is anything more that we can do now. I want to warn you that there is a dangerous killer loose. How are your guns? In good working order? Here, let me inspect them before you go out. I don't want you to take any chances."

The four policemen presented their revolvers for the Sergeant's examination. He made a careful inspection of each piece. While he was thus occupied, Blatchly turned to Trout and asked, "Got any idea why anybody would want to bump you off?"

Trout looked at him curiously, then smiled and answered, "I am glad you asked me that question, Joe. The only reason I can think of at present, is that the killer must have an idea that we know a great deal more than we do about him. If he knew how little we actually know or are likely to know, he would not be going about wasting valuable ammunition on us."

Cusani, finding the guns in order, returned them to their owners, whom he sent back to their posts.

Trout asked Mather to wait a moment while he explained to him about the guard which had been placed over him. "You see, Bill, it was to prevent the very thing that was attempted here from happening to you. It was only through the sheerest luck that I chanced to look at the window when I did."

"Thank you, Percy, but why should any one want me out of the way?"

"I think that he is getting panicky when he almost slipped up on Redfield . . . Left without making sure that he had quieted him for good . . . He took no chances on Romano . . . I am sure that he was ready to do the same for others whom he thought might know something . . . By the way, I talked to an old friend of ours this afternoon."

"Who was that?"

"You remember Dick Martin, don't you?"

"Dick Martin? Of course I do. Why Dick Martin . . . Good Heavens, Percy! . . . How very strange."

"What do you mean?"

"Why, Dick Martin is the only person I know, outside of us here, who knew Bert Somers' secret. He is the only one who knows who the girl was . . . He knows who her parents were."

"I think that it would be best if you told us the rest of it, Mather," suggested Trout.

"Yes," agreed the Dean. "I did not tell you before, because it never entered my mind that it could have any connection with the case. Martin was the one that brought Bert and the girl together. He himself was in love with her, but, after she met Somers, he did not have a chance . . . After she had gone, Martin came to see us one night . . . He was drunk . . . He accused us of kidnapping her. We did our best to sober him up and then told him the whole truth.

He appeared heartbroken, but agreed that we had acted in he
best interests. He promised that as long as she lived, he would kee
the secret intact . . . We saw very little of him after that. He b
came morose . . . Took to drinking heavily. We met him sever
years ago in New York. He was abusive to Somers. From some r
marks he made we inferred that he had seen her again in Franc
It is a strange coincidence that he should turn up at this time

"I don't believe in coincidences of that kind," remarked Trou
tersely.

When Mather had gone, Cusani sighed. "What a day! It seen
as though it was a year ago when we found Redfield dead instea
of a few hours, and since then, another killing and an attempt
still another one. Nor are we a bit further advanced as far as
can see."

"Oh, yes we are. This time, at least, we have caught a glimp
of the killer."

"You saw him?" exclaimed Cusani excitedly. "Did you get
good look at him?"

"Merely a glimpse. I saw the gun plainly . . . It was leveled d
rectly at me."

"Couldn't you identify him at all, Major? Make out any of h
features?"

"No more than a glimpse, as I said. But . . ." he hesitated, "I g
a strange impression . . . Don't think me fanciful . . . I know,
course, that it is impossible . . . But the flashing glimpse was of
face that we both have seen."

"Who was it?" whispered Cusani breathlessly.

"John Redfield."

There was a dead silence as Cusani gazed at Trout aghast. T
Sergeant was about to speak, then raised his hand uncertainly
his lips as he stared intently at the Major . . . And then the tru
came to him . . . He knew who the killer was and why Judge Sor
ers had to die! . . . It burst on him like a vivid flash of blindir
light.

CHAPTER 1{

"BUT THE PROOF, PERCY. The proof. We know who
is and we know the motive, but we haven't any proc
We can't go to a jury with such a story. Why, if I went
the State's Attorney with a request for prosecution on such groun
he would send me to the examining board to see if I was all there

"Don't worry your head about the proofs, Sally. I will have them all for you by tomorrow noon. It's an airtight case. With the evidence which we had in our hands Thursday, we should have made an arrest. We did not interpret it correctly. It is getting late and I still have some planning to do before I go to bed. I can foresee another tough day tomorrow. But we will finish it up. There are some things I would like to have you do now. Before you turn in, check up on the guard at Prexy's. Then I want you to wait a minute while I make out a list of names."

He took a sheet of paper and wrote hurriedly. After checking it carefully, he handed it to the Sergeant.

"Will you please arrange for all these persons to be at Chief Donovan's office at headquarters at two o'clock tomorrow, or I should say, this afternoon? Tell them that it is important, that we are going to have a conference and that we need their presence. I do not need to tell you that under no circumstances is any one to be told what we know until the proper time arrives. You yourself, take care that you do not by any action, word or look betray what is in your mind. It's after two o'clock now and in twelve hours it will be all over. Goodby and watch your step."

When the detective had gone, Trout sat at the table thinking deeply and making notes. After some time he began a self-catechization.

"When Mather was with the Judge, where was the killer?"

"Nearby."

"When Redfield was with the Judge, where was the killer?"

"Nearby."

"When Romano was with the Judge, where was the killer?"

"Nearby."

"When Mather, Redfield and Romano left the Judge, where was the killer?"

"Nearby."

"When Mather returned from his rooms and Redfield came across the campus after having paid the finance man, where was the killer?"

"Right there. They must have seen him."

"Why didn't they say anything?"

"Because he was beyond suspicion . . . It's strange how the human mind works. Here is a red-handed murderer and because of his position in life, no one suspected him. Murder is not like any other crime. Some persons would commit murder who would shrink from petty larceny . . . Now in the Redfield case it is much simpler. Where was the murderer?"

"From nine-thirty until about ten o'clock, he was in Redfield's room. Redfield must have known and trusted him. Can I prove that?"

"Yes."

"Who was the tall man?"

"I will know tomorrow. That's easy. I wish it was all as simple as that . . . Now for the Romano butchery . . . Where was the killer when Blatchly did his talking?"

"Nearby."

"Did Dick Martin see him?"

"Maybe. It is of no importance. But he knew who it was . . . Yes, he knew."

He closed his eyes and concentrated.

"Yes, it all checks. Everything clicks into its proper place. How could we have been so blind? Tomorrow then . . . Perhaps three calls for the tall man, call at headquarters, call at city clerk's office, call at Davenport's, call at Fernaud's, and all before two o'clock. A busy day is right."

He went to bed and was asleep without knowing that Cusani had stationed a policeman to guard his door.

After a hasty breakfast next morning, Trout called for his car and started out on his errands. His first call was at an office building where he spent a few minutes only. The next was at the plant of a large public service company, in the outskirts of the city. His visit there took longer, but when he left, he was wearing a satisfied smile.

At eleven o'clock, Trout was mounting the steps to police headquarters. He had a chat with Sergeant Lonergan and went in to Chief Donovan's office. The old man was a pitiful picture. He looked up as Trout entered, a look of despair in his kindly eyes, his haggard features drawn and woe-begone.

"Cheer up, Chief," said Trout heartily. "You look as though you had lost your last friend."

"You would, too, Professor, if you had been through what I have."

"What's the trouble?"

"The Mayor has just left. They are going to take the investigation out of our hands. For myself I don't care much. I am about through anyway, but it will break Sally's heart. I don't know how I'm going to tell him."

"If you haven't told him yet, don't."

"But some one has got to tell him before three o'clock. The state troopers are going to take it over then. The Mayor said he was going to call the Governor right away. He's probably done it by this time. What can I do?"

"Sit tight, Chief. Somebody is due for a surprise. Did you think that Sally was just running around doing nothing?"

"I guess you ain't seen the papers yet, Professor."

"No, I haven't had time." Then sensing that there was more to the Chief's demeanor than he had shown, asked, "Why? Was there anything that I should have noticed particularly?"

Donovan handed him the local sheet and pointing to a paragraph, said dismally, "Read that."

Trout ran his eyes casually over a vituperative article which scored the police from the head down. It accused the organization of inefficiency and blundering in the Somers case and hinted at something unsavory and dark in the other killings.

He glanced at the worried Donovan and said, "That is pretty raw, Chief, but don't let it get under your skin too deeply. We will make them eat their own words in a few hours, and as for the state police, much as I admire their efficiency, I am afraid that this time they will be too late."

"Do you mean that, Professor?" said Donovan hopefully. "You ain't kidding me to make me feel good?"

"Don't breathe a word but sit tight. I suppose that Sally has told you that we are going to hold a meeting of the witnesses this afternoon."

He walked over to a large glass case against the wall and examined the contents carefully. He nodded and smiled quietly. "Check and double check. I knew it! There yesterday, and gone today."

He turned back to the Chief and said, "With such a fine display of mementoes of previous convictions as are gathered in that cabinet, you have nothing to fear from those irresponsible charges. I should think that you would keep it locked up though."

"Why? There ain't nothing valuable in it."

"Souvenir hunters, Chief. Keep your chin up. I must be on my way."

He waved a cheerful farewell and went out on his next errand. That was to the office of the city clerk. He spent an hour there examining records, some of which were more than forty years old, before he found what he wanted.

"It couldn't be otherwise," he murmured. "If we had only thought of that before."

He entered his car and drove slowly, meditating to President Davenport's home.

"Come in, Dr. Trout," said Davenport when Adams had escorted him to the library door. "Come in. I was about to light a cigar. Will you join me?"

Trout declined, and Davenport smiled as he said, "I have some better ones than these that I am smoking, but I prefer this local brand. The tobacco is much lighter and they are easier on my throat. You will find some good Havanas in the humidor."

Trout shook his head and said, "No, thank you, Dr. Davenport. I know that you are anxious for me to clear up the murder of our good friend, Judge Somers. We have made some progress and we are now at a point where it seems advisable to hold a meeting of all witnesses and any others who may be able to throw light on the matter. I believe that any one who knew the Judge well should be there also. Some points may arise that could be answered without tedious delays. I am, therefore, hoping that you will be at police headquarters at two o'clock this afternoon."

"Certainly, you may count on me."

"Thank you, sir. There have been many anxieties and perplexities in this case. Three men have met sudden death and an attempt was made on my life last night."

"You astound me, Trout. I had heard that there was some disturbance on your campus, but I had no idea that it was as serious as that."

"I wonder how the information reached you?"

"Through one of the proctors, I believe. I cannot recall who it was."

"It does not matter. Dean Mather was there, and with the help of one of the students, we were able to restore order without much trouble."

The conversation turned to the murders again. After a half hour talk Trout took his departure.

It was one o'clock when he drew up at the Fernaud house. He noticed Cusani's car parked at the curb and smiled. Thelma admitted him. On seeing him she became confused and said, "I didn't know you was a college professor, Mr. Trout. I thought you was one of them cops. You must of thought that I was pretty fresh yesterday kidding with you like I did. Miss Elsie gave me an awful calling down."

"I am sorry, Thelma. Here, take this . . . When you get a chance, go to a good movie. I am sure you will find some nice young chap to keep you company. I would like to see Miss Fernaud if she is not busy."

"She's in there with that Eyetalian cop. I'll go tell her that you are here."

Elsie greeted him cordially.

"Sergeant Cusani has told me about the meeting this afternoon. Of course I will come if I can be of any help, but I am afraid that there is no more that I can tell you."

"Thank you. I would like you to be there. I have asked every one who has had any connection with the case, to be present. Some question may arise and could be answered at once if everybody is at hand. Is there anything that I can do regarding Redfield's funeral?"

"No, thank you. Dean Mather has taken over all the arrangements. He has been most kind and considerate."

"I can believe that. There is, however, one question that I would like to ask. You will remember that you told us that when you returned from your marketing and found Redfield's visitor was still with him, you took up your household duties. I wonder if you heard any sounds in the cellar? I notice that the cellar stairs lead from the hall and unless you happened to be there, you would be unable to see any one going to or from the cellar. Did you hear any one?"

"Yes, I did. It was a short time before the door slammed. I thought at the time that it was Thelma and wondered what she was doing there. Of course, the tragedy afterward drove everything else out of my mind and I forgot to mention it. I am sorry."

"No harm done, Miss Elsie. I would like a few words with you, Sally, before the meeting. Will you meet me in my rooms for lunch?"

CHAPTER 19

DONOVAN'S ROOMY OFFICE was well but not uncomfortably filled at two o'clock Tuesday afternoon. The Chief sat at his desk flanked on one side by Trout, on the other by Cusani. Ranged about the room standing, were Blatchly, Finn and Maloney of the uniformed force, while seated were Miss Fernaud, Thelma, President Davenport, Dean Mather, Bob Somers, Gregory, and a tall slim man in a dark uniform.

There was a tenseness of avid excitement in the atmosphere, an uneasiness as each one present stirred nervously.

Professor Trout stood up. There was an expectant hush. He looked around at those there as if to check everyone, then satisfied that no one was missing, addressed them clearly in his peculiar, high pitched voice.

"We have come to a stage in our investigations where we must clear the innocent of all suspicion and point the finger of guilt at the person who is responsible for the cowardly killing of three human beings. Sergeant Cusani has gathered incontestable proof that will send a person, now in this room, to the electric chair."

There was a murmur and a movement in his audience as some looked at their neighbors askance and others stared at the Major. From somewhere in the room came a deep sigh. Trout continued. "The Sergeant in his modest way, has asked me to apologize to you for any inconvenience he may have put you to and to thank you for your co-operation. He also feels that had he taken certain precautions sooner, two lives may have been saved. I do not agree with him. It was impossible to foresee what was about to happen."

He paused and looked at the ceiling, his hands in his coat pockets, as he continued, "With the exception of some of the police, every one in this room has been at some time or other, during the past five days, under direct suspicion. You will note that I said 'some of the police' . . . You, Blatchly, and you too, Finn, have not been entirely free from suspicion . . . Let me run over the list of suspects with you.

"We will dispose of the police first. Blatchly, we find, was in close proximity of the last crime, the killing of Romano. He was heard to make threats and certain remarks that could easily pin that murder on him. He reported late yesterday morning . . . Just before the alarm of Redfield's murder reached headquarters. He knew Redfield and could have been Redfield's morning visitor. Redfield was frightened of the police . . . Of the very methods Blatchly threatened to employ . . . Redfield's last breath accused the police of using those methods. The situation looked very black for Blatchly, except that Sergeant Cusani has decided that all three murders are tied together . . . The work of one hand . . . So Joe Blatchly may be counted out. He has an unassailable alibi for the murder of Judge Somers. He was here at headquarters with Chief Donovan and Cusani at the time the Judge was killed.

"The next of the police suspects is Patrolman Finn. He was in close proximity and at the correct time for the Judge's murder. He was here on the scene of the Romano killing yesterday afternoon, but yesterday morning he was walking his beat. We have the hourly reports from his call-box and he was not relieved until noon, when he came here with the rest of his relief. He knew Redfield well. His beat included Redfield's post and they often stopped to chat.

"Redfield and Romano, of course, were suspects for the first killing, but they could not have committed the other crimes. Another suspect whom we will dispose of quickly is now in the county jail. He could have broken this case for us Thursday. He is responsible for all three murders, although he did not commit any of them. His murky mind even now does not know what his vindictive tongue has done."

Trout paused, and picking his words with care, proceeded, "We will now take up the others in this room. I am compelled to make my remarks directly personal. I repeat that with the few exceptions which I have mentioned, you all came under suspicion. Even you, Bob Somers. But your absence in New York yesterday absolves you. Remember one person and only one perpetrated all the murders. Mr. Gregory also came under the cloud, but in clearing Somers, he too is absolved automatically.

"Miss Fernaud could have caused Redfield's death. She was present at the place and time, but she could not have killed Judge Somers or Romano. The same conditions apply to Thelma Andersen. There is present here at my request a Mr. James Hunt." Trout indicated the tall stranger.

"Mr. Hunt was for a time under suspicion in the Redfield case. He was seen to leave the house hurriedly shortly after that killing. He is an employee of the Gas Light Company. He came to the house to take a corrected meter reading. He found the front door open and walked in . . . Took the reading with the aid of the electric torch he carried with him in the cellar . . . Slammed the front door on his way out to insure its closing and drove away in one of his company's cars."

Trout paused again as he surveyed his tense listeners. "And now," he continued with a kindly smile, "we come to my old friend Dean Mather. The Dean was an outstanding suspect for two of the murders. A net of circumstantial evidence was spun around him that would have convinced any jury of his guilt. He had the opportunities, the time and what might have been construed as a powerful motive for the killing of Judge Somers and John Redfield. Sergeant Cusani, however, wisely refrained from making the arrest. It was impossible for the Dean to have done the third killing. At the time of Romano's death, Dean Mather was with Cusani and myself in my rooms. He is, therefore, absolved."

Trout waited a much longer period as his eyes rested on each of his auditors before he went on. An expression of sorrow and pity came over his rough-hewn features and there was a break in his voice.

"You may think it peculiar that we should, even for a moment, have considered that a man of Dean Mather's standing could be guilty of such terrible crimes. Murder is not confined to any one class. In many cases murder, which most of us consider the greatest crime against society and therefore the crime which carries with it the maximum penalty, is the first and only crime that the murderer has perpetrated. That is why it is so difficult to solve in some cases. We look for a reason, a motive. In most other crimes—theft, rape, kidnapping, sabotage, treason or libel—the motive is fairly evident and usually contemporary with the performance of the act. In cases of murder the motive may be one of many and the cause may have existed for a long time. In this case, the roots of the motive are sunk deeply in the dim past. I am sure you will pardon me for this apparent digression. I wanted to impress on you that in cases of murder the sex, social position, occupation, age or previous deportment of the murderer may mislead the investigators. Several well-known cases come to mind. King David, the schoolmaster Aram, the policeman Becker, the widow Judith, Ruth Snyder, Dr. Crippen, those two boys in Chicago, the friar Jacques Clement, Cain and the noble Brutus were all guilty. Would any one have believed before the deed was accomplished, that murder, cold-blooded and premeditated, lurked in their hearts? This, therefore, is our justification for even the slightest suspicions we may have had against you, Dr. Davenport. It seemed so improbable that you could have done these horrible crimes . . . Yet, you were in the vicinity when Judge Somers was killed and in the same building when Romano met his death. At the time of the Redfield murder you were not at your home or office."

"But, Dr. Trout, I told you that I was taking a walk yesterday morning!" exclaimed the dignified executive.

"Yes, Dr. Davenport, you did tell me that. I do not doubt your word. I do not think there is anything more that I want to say. I believe that we have cleared the innocent. Everything is quite clear to us. We know who the murderer is and Sergeant Cusani will make the arrest."

Cusani rose and took a shining pair of handcuffs from his pocket. He stood for a moment in silence as if hesitating how to proceed, then spoke quietly.

"There may be a struggle and as there are so many in this room, some one may be hurt. I want to make sure that there will be no more sudden deaths. The killer can be taken without bloodshed and I therefore will ask the police to place their guns on this desk here before we go any further . . . Blatchly, your gun please . . . Thank you . . . Yours Maloney . . . Thanks . . Yours Finn . . . Thanks. What's that in your other hand?"

"Nothing." Finn showed his empty palm.

There was a quick move, a click, and Cusani stepped aside. With a wave of his hand he announced dramatically.

"Ladies and Gentlemen, I introduce Patrick Finn, the triple killer."

CHAPTER 20

TROUT, MATHER AND CUSANI were seated at a table in an Italian restaurant. It was late and they had the place to themselves. They had finished an excellent meal and a bottle of strega had been left on the table. Trout was speaking. "So they decided to let Martin go. There was nothing else to do. He promised to keep quiet. Now there will be no need to tell Somers' secret to the world."

"Yeah, that's right," said Cusani. "What's that they always say about the dead? . . . You know what I mean. And now, Major, what do you say to satisfying the Dean's curiosity, and I might add mine, too. There are a lot of details you haven't told me yet, you know."

"Such as?"

"The confab you, Finn and Chief Donovan had in the Chief's office after the arrest . . . Finn said he wouldn't talk to any one but you and the Chief. Did you get a confession?"

"Yes, we did," said Trout soberly. "It was pretty ghastly . . . The end especially . . . Perhaps I had better give you the whole story as he told it. I don't think that it will be necessary to go into the metaphysical end. The dissection and analyzation of a mind which for many years was absorbed with one thought, one idea. A life of frustrated hopes dedicated to revenge."

Trout refilled his glass and took a sip of the viscous liquid. He went on slowly, "There is a verse in Proverbs which I will quote. Its application will be apparent shortly. 'There is a way which seemeth right unto a man, but the end thereof are the ways of death.' . . . When Finn asked for a private interview with the Chief and myself, I knew that his object was to entreat us to keep his daughter's name and reputation from becoming public property. That we promised to do if it was at all possible. He told us how his daughter left her home. He verified the whole story that Mather told us. He and his wife had great ambitions for the girl. Martin had inspired them . . . They thought that he would marry her, and saw their daughter installed in a family of refinement and wealth. For themselves they asked nothing, for her, everything. They idolized her; she was their whole, their one and all. Then they noticed that she had cooled toward Martin and from several remarks, gathered that some one else had taken his place. Then came her trouble . . . She left them. They never knew who the man was. They did know it was not Martin. The mother died at the end of the first year . . . He said that she died of a broken heart. That changed his whole life . . . He was alone in the world . . . His spiritual props had been taken from him. Almost nothing of the man was left . . . He degenerated mentally to the level of an animal . . . Revenge and the instinct of self-preservation. I wonder if I have made the picture clear to you?"

His companions nodded silently. Trout went on with his story. "Now Dick Martin comes in again. Whether or not he made a trip here for the object of telling Finn who betrayed his daughter, or whether in his talk with Somers on the train, something was said which spurred him to reveal the secret, we will never know. Finn said he came to tell him that the girl had died and during the conversation the story slipped out. Maybe that is the charitable way to look at it although I doubt it. Personally I am of the opinion that Martin did it deliberately. However, the speculation is idle and useless. It's time for some one to ring in the platitude Sally was trying to remember."

He took another sip from his glass.

"Now this is what happened, this is the way Finn told it. After his talk with Martin, he reported for duty and was assigned to the east portal of the old campus. He was there when Redfield made the appointment and like Romano, overheard the conversation. Redfield left him and he waited for his return, but Redfield did not return. He became anxious . . . He was afraid he would lose his opportunity. He determined to wait no longer and went. If any one saw him he could say that he was looking for Redfield. He approached the room cautiously, exactly as Romano described it to Sally. When he entered, the room was empty, but he heard some one at the wash-bowl in the bathroom . . . He called out and Somers came out into the doorway . . . He drew his gun. Somers made a rush at him and he shot him . . . No warning . . . No word of any kind . . . Simply shot him down . . . He died instantly. Finn stooped over him, the smoking revolver in his hand. The hat was lying there on the floor and on the rug was the bullet. He picked it up. He said that it was so hot that it almost burnt him . . . He gave it to Donovan . . . A souvenir, he said . . . Well, how does that check with my reconstruction?"

He refilled his glass and glanced quizzically at Mather and Sally.

"Yeah, we know you are pretty good, Major," said Cusani. "What about the rest of it?"

"After killing Somers, he went downstairs and out on the campus. As he was walking back to his post, he saw Redfield hurrying across the campus. Both arrived at the portal at the same time. Redfield asked Finn where he had been and Finn thought that he had put him off by saying that he had gone in to keep order. Sunday evening, while on his beat, Finn was approached by Redfield with a request for a loan of fifty dollars . . . This is how Finn tells it. 'I haven't got it, Johnny.' Redfield said, 'You better find it, Pat, and bring it over to the house tomorrow morning. There's going to be a lot of questions asked about where you were when Judge Somers was shot.' . . . Finn made an appointment to meet him between nine and ten. He was on the eight to twelve detail morning and night. He reported from his call-box at nine . . . Went over to Redfield's, was admitted to the house by Redfield, who was waiting for him in the hall, and went into Redfield's room . . . They sat down . . . Finn lighted a cigar and Redfield a cigarette . . . Redfield told him that Somers' death had cut off his income . . . That he saw Finn coming out of the section entry and that he thought Finn owed him a regular revenue . . . He kept stressing the point that as Finn had deprived him of his income, Finn should restore it . . .

Of course Redfield knew nothing of Bert's will . . . All that he had in mind at any time was the money that Somers furnished him, and all that Somers' death meant to him was the loss of that money. He was not a nice person . . . When he had finished his argument, Finn leaned over to flick his cigar ash into the tray. Redfield was just lighting a cigarette . . . Finn took the opportunity presented; dropped his cigar and slid his hands down on the pedestal of the stand; jumped up before Redfield could divine his purpose and swung the stand with a crashing blow on the back of his head. He ran out silently and swiftly, left the front door open lest some sound might betray him and was back on his beat at 10:04 . . . The time he reported from his call-box. Close enough to establish an alibi. However, our match trick broke that . . . How does that check with the reconstruction?"

"I told you that you were good, Percy," said Cusani.

"I know damn well that I am," chuckled Trout. "Listen to this. This is the way Romano passed out . . . When Finn was relieved, he went to headquarters with the rest of the First Precinct men in his squad. They stood around gossiping. Blatchly came from the cell corridor and did his talking . . . Finn, certain that he had destroyed all evidence against himself by eliminating Redfield, found himself with another witness on his hands. At that moment, Elmer, the fingerprint man, came back and told them that Redfield had not died at once . . . Well, the rest was not difficult . . . Finn went into the corridor, a natural thing to do . . . The washroom was there . . . He took the cell key. It was as Martin told us . . . This time, however, he would make certain . . . It was rather horrible the way he told it; dispassionately, as if he was telling about a rat-killing . . . If he had known that Martin was awake he would have killed him too. He said so . . . When it was over he went into the washroom and cleaned himself. The damp spots barely showed on his dark-blue uniform . . . Well, how about the reconstruction?"

"Pretty good," said Cusani negligently.

"Pretty good?" snorted Trout. "Perfect, you mean."

"Okay. Call it perfect if you want to. You don't hate yourself much. Do you? But go on. We want to hear the rest of it."

Trout filled his glass, took a sip, smacked his lips and continued. "This is the most unpleasant part of it . . . But, after all it may turn out for the best . . . When Finn completed his confession, Chief Donovan said, 'Then no one told you, Pat, that Redfield was your grandson?' . . . I could have choked him . . . The reaction was frightful. Finn turned white as a sheet and whispered, 'Did I kill Loretta's kid?' Donovan nodded. I could see a change come over Finn as he sat there silently. His face became suffused with blood; it grew darker and darker until he was almost purple; his eyes became bloodshot. For a moment I thought he was suffering from a stroke, and then he began to laugh, shrill, high and unnatural. He became violent. It was all Donovan and I could do to hold him until you and Lonergan came in . . . Mansfield and I have certified him as insane. Of course he will be examined by a commission . . . He will probably outlive us all. I never saw a man of his age in better physical condition . . . Well men, that's the whole story."

"Thank you, Percy," said Dean Mather. "I wonder if you would care to tell me how you and Cusani arrived at your conclusions?"

"He's dying to tell you, Dean. If you hadn't asked him, he would have had a grouch for a week."

Trout gave Sally the expressive salute which Dr. Frederick A. Johnson described some years ago in hexameter, "With thumb on the nose and fingers extended in the way of the ancient Egyptians," and turned to Mather. "I thought it was all pretty clear, Bill. What do you want me to tell you?"

"When did you first suspect Finn?"

"He was one of the first on my list. Do you remember the 'Red Mike and Violets' incident? I wondered at the time why he was so anxious to avoid questioning. Late for his dinner. Bah! The man was an athlete in splendid training. Do you remember how he ran away? Why should a policeman want to avoid questioning and get away from the scene of a serious crime? No, Finn was not the type to be thinking of his belly. There was some other reason."

"Yes, I can see that. What else?"

"There was the Redfield killing. Redfield's mumbled words to Miss Fernaud. I told Sally then that they were paragogic."

"Sure you did, Major," admitted Cusani. "I thought that was something they gave kids to make them go to sleep."

Trout laughed until tears came to his eyes. "Sally, as I have said before, I don't know what I would do without you. Look it up sometime . . . Look it up."

"I see now," said Mather. "What Redfield was trying to tell Miss Fernaud became muddled by the pressure against his brain.

"Yes. What he said was, 'It is Finn. The cop Finn.' The sibilation was the result of the pressure on his cerebellum, or rather, Pons Varolii. In the Rolandic region."

"I'll bet you are right," said Sally.

Trout looked at him doubtfully for a moment, but continued, "When I checked the time between Redfield's home and Finn's beat, I found that he could do it easily and make the call, if he left Redfield's a few minutes before ten o'clock. He had no alibi for the Redfield murder."

He paused to sip at his glass and addressed Cusani.

"When Miss Elsie described Redfield, Sally, didn't it occur to you that she also was describing Finn? Redfield was reminding you constantly of some one. It was not until last night, when Finn left my rooms, that you made the association. I didn't want to influence you . . . I wanted you to reach the conclusion entirely independently. I saw no one at the window . . . Only the gun. By the way, the muffler on that gun came out of Chief Donovan's cabinet. I saw it there yesterday, and it was missing this morning. Finn told us that he took it before he went on duty last night. It was the one that 'Big Mike Manetta' owned. He put it on the gun you found in the arm-holster when you searched him at headquarters after the arrest. That talk about Redfield's ghost last night was an act on my part."

"I see," said Cusani thoughtfully. "There was another act you pulled too. When I was examining the guns you told Blatchly that we had no idea who the killer was and that we had no hopes of catching him. You did that to lead Finn away from us, didn't you?"

"Elementary, my dear, Sally."

"Where was Finn hiding when we ran out on the campus last night?"

"We should have been prepared for that. He took a leaf from Romano's book. When he fired the shot at us, he slipped into my section entry and hid behind the door."

"But wasn't he taking a big chance in returning to the room?" asked Mather.

"No. If we had caught him there, he could have easily excused his presence . . . Had heard a disturbance . . . Came in to investigate . . . He could have given any number of reasons. He had seen Cusani's car and came in to consult him about some fictitious matter . . . He gave me several reasons he would have used had we interrogated him. We are losing sight of the fact that he was a well-known policeman in uniform, who had an unusual entree and who was normally above suspicion."

"If you knew he did it, why didn't you ask for his arrest sooner?" inquired the Dean.

"But I did not know. I had strong suspicions, but no actual knowledge. What was the motive? It was not until Sunday night, when you told me Somers' story, that I could work out any motivating compulsion behind the Judge's killing. What reason had I to pin that on Finn?"

"Well, there was the likeness between him and Redfield," commented Cusani.

"True enough. But you must remember that I had seen Finn only once before and that for only a moment at the portal. It was not until last night that I had time to make a good examination of his features."

"Anyway," said Sally, "that wasn't evidence. We couldn't go before a jury with that kind of bunk."

"That's true. Nor could we go to court with a few mumbled words of a dying man which were open to various interpretations. As a matter of fact, up to the time of Romano's murder we had a much better case against you, Bill. Opportunity, motive and means."

Mather nodded gravely and said, "I thank you both for your consideration."

"Romano's death," continued Trout, "was our best sign-post. But even then, I had no real evidence. I asked myself why, if Finn knew that Somers had betrayed the girl, did he wait for more than twenty years for his act of retribution? Mather supplied us with the answer last night when we told him about Dick Martin. Finn did not know until Thursday at about noon and in six hours Bert Somers was dead."

"Why did you not arrest him last night?" asked Mather.

"I did not have the complete evidence even then. This morning I went to the city clerk's office and searched the vital statistics. I found the record of Finn's marriage, the birth of his daughter, the death of his wife, but no record of the daughter's death. The records were quite complete . . . Most New England records are. I could have gone further. I could have found Finn's family physician. The same man who attended the girl's birth, certified to the wife's death. He is still living here in the city and without doubt was the doctor who discovered the girl's condition. But that was not necessary. I had all the evidence that we needed."

"But why did you have that meeting in Chief Donovan's office today?" asked Mather. "Why not arrest him quietly?"

Cusani grinned widely.

Trout gave a little embarrassed cough.

"You would not understand, Bill," he said . . . "Sally, you zoomp Pass the vanity."

www.ingramcontent.com/pod-product-compliance
Lightning Source LLC
Chambersburg PA
CBHW020151180626
46810CB00004B/1845